Totally Bound Publishing books by Aurora Russell

Anywhere and Always
Falling for the Tycoon

I0571298

THE AU PAIR
AND THE BEAST

AURORA RUSSELL

The Au Pair and the Beast
ISBN # 978-1-83943-949-0
©Copyright Aurora Russell 2021
Cover Art by Louisa Maggio ©Copyright February 2021
Interior text design by Claire Siemaszkiewicz
Totally Bound Publishing

THE AU PAIR
AND THE BEAST

Dedication

For my very own beast, and for our two beautiful, energetic, silly-billy boys. Also, for the rest of my wonderful family and friends, but especially for my dad and stepmother, my biggest fans and supporters in everything I do. Finally, for my brother and my sister-in-law. We may have always been meant to be family, but I'm so grateful we chose to be friends too.

Chapter One

"Wait... He's sending his own car and *driver* to pick you up from the train station? And take you to his *castle*? How deliciously Gothic! It's probably set high up on some cliffs, overlooking an impossibly picturesque view of waves crashing onto the rocks."

Veronica quirked her lips into a smile at Katrin's words as they crackled through her cell phone, the reception seeming to go in and out as she rode along. Her best friend had a pronounced flair for the dramatic, which had only been enhanced by a number of drama classes in college.

"Well, when you put it that way...it *does* sound pretty glamorous," she laughingly agreed. "If it looks anything like that, I'll definitely text a picture of the view, complete with fog and sea spray."

Her friend's answering chuckle was amused. "How does Madame Montreaux know this guy again?"

Thinking back on it, Veronica wasn't sure the woman who led her French conversation group had ever actually told her...not specifically, anyway.

"Weird. I'm not really sure… She just pulled me aside after our group one day and mentioned she'd heard about a job she thought I might be perfect for, you know, since she knew I'd lost my job when Dumfries & Partners was acquired. I got the impression—maybe just from her voice or something?—that he's some sort of family friend, but she was super skimpy on details." She drummed her fingers on her armrest as she considered. "I had to sign a confidentiality agreement before they even sent me the job description."

"Hmm-m." The one short word seemed filled with both skepticism and suspicion. "How old are the kids?"

"Just one child. A boy. I think he's four… Not in school yet, but he goes to preschool."

Veronica watched as the increasingly rural and wooded landscape flew by outside the window. The day was gray and dreary, but the beauty of the wilds of Maine was still undeniable. The well-modulated, incongruously feminine automated voice of the announcer came over the loudspeakers.

"Next stop, Grant's Cliff. Grant's Cliff is a flagged stop. Please notify the conductor if you are getting off at this stop."

Excitement and nerves combined into one powerful spark that set off a flurry of butterflies in Veronica's stomach, even as she stood and started to gather up her things.

"Sorry, K… Gotta go. They just called my stop. Call you later, okay?"

"Yes! Call, text, everything… I'll be waiting impatiently to hear that you haven't been chained up in this guy's basement—or dungeon. Whatever. Be careful! And good luck!"

Cradling the phone between her shoulder and cheek as she reached for her bag from the overhead storage,

Veronica barked a laugh, and it was muffled. "Thank you?"

"Anytime! Bye!"

"Bye," Veronica answered, letting her bag drop into the seat and clicking to end the call on her phone. And it seemed it wasn't a moment too soon as she caught the conductor's eye and the train began to slow. She'd told him earlier where she was getting off and she was glad she had, since it didn't look like anyone else on the train was making a move to leave. Grant's Cliff was apparently not a popular destination.

"Right this way, miss." The conductor's weathered face creased into a kindly smile as he motioned her with one work-hardened hand.

"Thanks." She gave an answering grin and slipped the strap of her suitcase over her shoulder crosswise, sliding it to her back so she could hurry down the center aisle more easily. "Am I the only one getting off?"

"A-yup," he said, his Maine accent plain. She thought that was all he'd say, but as she stepped out of the open door onto the small platform, she heard him add, "Not much out here nowadays, apart from the castle and the beast."

Startled, she turned back, but the doors had already swished closed and the train began to pull away. *Okay then.*

She turned back and surveyed the deserted station. It was really more of a booth set next to a concrete slab platform with steps leading up to it. The metal sign for the station name was no bigger than a street sign and looked weathered. The dreary day had given way to fog, and now that the train had left, the only sound was the muffled rustling of the wind through thousands of trees. *Where the heck is the driver?* she wondered. Even as she looked around, half of her mind was still on the conductor's strange words. *What did he mean by the beast? Why hasn't anyone else mentioned it? Is this, like, a hotspot for sasquatch hunters? Or the home of a rogue grizzly? Wait! Are there even grizzly bears in Maine?* She thought maybe there were only black bears. But still, a rogue black bear could definitely be a beast.

When someone's gentle hand touched her shoulder, pulling her from her thoughts, she screeched and jumped what felt like three feet off the ground.

"Mademoiselle Carson? Veronica Carson?" The middle-aged man's accent was unmistakably French, and he pronounced her first name as *Vehr-oh-nee-ka.* She quickly raised her hand to her neck where her pulse was still racing.

"Yes," she nodded, a little breathless. "So sorry. I didn't hear anyone."

The man, who she noticed now was wearing a dark suit and even a driver's hat, smiled understandingly. "The fog. When it is thick like this, well...everything is hushed."

"Of course, that makes sense." She was relieved at such a simple explanation.

He held out his hand formally. "Claude Hormet, in service to Monsieur Reynard for many years."

She held her hand to meet his, and it was immediately taken into a firm handshake. "Nice to meet you, Monsieur Hormet."

His smile widened at her pronunciation of his name, and she thought she saw surprise flicker in his eyes. "It's a pleasure to meet you as well, Mademoiselle. We were told you spoke French well, and I can already hear it, if you don't mind my saying so."

"Thank you. That's very kind of you. I'm happy to switch over if you'd like, so you can really hear me."

Monsieur Hormet smiled again. "I would enjoy that, but later. For now, I will escort you to the château."

He took her bag from her and led her to a shiny, black Lincoln sedan that looked pristine in spite of the fact that it must have been at least thirty years old. He opened the back door, and once she'd slid onto the back seat, he gave a little bow before closing the door behind her. She didn't even hear the trunk close after he'd put her suitcase in, and when they began to move, the ride was so smooth that it felt like they were floating.

Monsieur Hormet didn't speak again, and sensing that it would possibly be considered too informal for her to initiate conversation, Veronica maintained silence as well. Instead, she took out her folder with a copy of her resume and list of references. She reviewed her notes again, but they were sparse. From the barebones details that had accompanied the job description, she really didn't know a lot about the open position and still didn't know anything more about her prospective employer than his last name, so she rehearsed again in her head what she could say about her experience.

She was so deep in thought, comfortable on the sumptuous leather of the seats, that she didn't really look up until the car began to slow. Then...*wow*. The mansion that loomed before her was truly a castle, made of stone with towers and turrets. If it had had a moat and not located in Maine, she would not have been surprised if someone had told her it was from the Middle Ages.

She must have made some sort of sound because Monsieur Hormet caught her gaze in the rearview mirror.

"Ah, the château is beautiful, no?"

Looking back at the lines of the massive structure, Veronica noticed that they were surprisingly delicate as well. Large it might be, but this was also a masterpiece of artistry, balanced and elegant. Still trying to look at every part of the castle at the same time, she answered with enthusiasm, "Oh yes, absolutely gorgeous!"

They pulled up right to the front steps, and Monsieur Hormet came around to help her out of the car. The air that buffeted her face was cooler than at the train station, damp and heavy, carrying the unmistakable salty tang of the ocean. She curved her lips into a small smile when she heard the distant crash of waves on something. Katrin was going to be overjoyed that her guess had to be at least partly correct.

"If you'll follow me, Mademoiselle, I'll show you to the large salon." Monsieur Hormet glanced at the front windows and nodded slightly at some small movement inside. "Eveline will let Monsieur Reynard know you've arrived."

Still craning her neck as discreetly as possible to see everything at once, Veronica followed him up a large number of stone steps and into the château. She had only a glimpse of the enormous entry hall before they went down a spacious hallway into a room that looked like some sort of formal parlor. There were several seating areas around the room, and he motioned for her to sit in a straight-backed armchair in the cluster nearest to the windows. Even with the fog, she could still tell that the windows here overlooked the ocean. A gray-green expanse of icy-cold Atlantic water, the view looked imposing rather than inviting. She loved it.

Fighting the urge to press her nose to the glass of the windowpanes, she sat down on the chair instead in what she hoped was a professional, dignified manner.

She took out the folder once again and waited. An ornate gilded clock, which looked like an antique that would have been at home in the art museum in Boston, ticked, and the sound was loud in the otherwise-silent room. At the *snick* of the door handle turning, she leaped to her feet and turned to greet her interviewer. The figure that entered was considerably shorter and faster than she'd expected, though.

As he barreled toward her at full tilt, Veronica saw that the little boy had a mass of golden-blond hair, bright blue eyes and cheeks that glowed pink with good health. His happy face was dominated by a huge grin. She braced for possible impact, but he stopped abruptly right in front of her and eyed her curiously.

"You're pretty," he said in French, "but I don't like your coat. I'm not supposed to say 'hate' or 'ugly'." He looked up at her expectantly.

Veronica stifled a laugh as she darted a glance down at her suit coat. It was something she'd bought for interviews, and she internally agreed that it wasn't the most attractive thing she owned—more about practicality than fashion. But still...

"It sounds like you're doing a good job listening, then," she answered in French, skirting around the question. She set her folder, which she'd still been clutching, on the seat of the chair and crouched down so she was eye-level with the boy. "What's your name? Mine is Veronica."

"Jean-Philippe. Yvette says you're here to take care of me, but only if Papa likes you. I don't have a *maman*. She died. Our dog died too. Sometimes I get sad and cry and Papa says that's okay." Veronica's heart clenched at the childish words, but she fought another laugh at what he said next. "Did you bring a present? Papa always brings a present and hides it in one of his pockets. *Oncle* Marius too. Is that why you're wearing that coat, to hide presents?" He eyed her outfit with more enthusiasm.

"It's a pleasure to meet you, Jean-Philippe," she answered, then shook her head regretfully. "I didn't know, so no presents today, but I promise that if I stay, I'll bring you something next time I go into town. How's that?"

He bobbed his little head as he nodded, making his fine blond hair glint, even in the dim sunlight from the gloomy day. "That sounds good," he agreed. "I hope you go to town soon."

She couldn't have hidden her smile this time if she'd tried, so she didn't bother. Another noise made her look up again, toward the door, where a young woman stood, looking a bit harried. Her chest rose and fell rapidly, as if she'd been running. She wore some sort of uniform dress, not black-and-white but something about it made Veronica think she might be a maid or housekeeper. Her look at Jean-Philippe was a mix of exasperation and affection.

The man who entered on her heels, though, made Veronica shoot to her feet and straighten her back. He was tall, probably close to six-and-a-half feet, and his shoulders and chest were broad and muscular. He wore a suit that must have been custom-tailored to fit his large frame so perfectly, and he exuded an air of pure power. Confidence. She would have had to be blind or utterly oblivious not to feel an awareness of such a man.

Where his frame and his very presence seemed to fill the room, it was his face that really captivated her. Dark, wavy hair framed the most attractive face she thought she'd ever seen. He wasn't what she would call handsome—his Roman nose was just a little too prominent—but his features were masculine, strong and absolutely stunning. His eyes, which she could tell even from this distance were a deep brown like melted dark chocolate and framed with thick dark lashes, seemed to see all the way into her from across the room. She felt goosebumps rise on her arms and up her neck, and she couldn't seem to tear her own gaze away.

When he started to move, whatever spell that was keeping her silent was broken. To her surprise, she noticed that he walked with a cane in steps that looked like they carefully concealed pain.

"Oh, Monsieur, I'm so sorry. He got away from me when he was supposed to be following me," the young woman apologized to the man who she guessed must be Monsieur Reynard.

He inclined his head slightly, and although his face remained impassive, Veronica somehow got the impression of tolerance.

"I understand, Yvette. You may return to your regular duties." His voice was deep and rumbling, full of gravel. It rolled through the quiet room, filling every corner, though he spoke quietly.

The young woman gave a little bow and hurried from the room gratefully, leaving only Veronica, Jean-Philippe and Monsieur Reynard.

"Papa!" the little boy exclaimed, confirming Veronica's guess at the identity of the man. She saw him grimace almost imperceptibly as his little boy crashed into his leg in a show of preschool affection.

"I see you've met Miss Carson, my son," he said, looking at Veronica as he tousled the baby-fine mop of hair.

"Oh yes! Do you like her? Is she staying?"

The question fell heavily in the quiet room, and Veronica turned to pick up the folder again.

"I brought a copy of my resume and a list of references —"

"No need." Monsieur Reynard interrupted her, gesturing with his hand as if to wave her words away. "I've seen enough. The job is yours."

Veronica's mouth fell open. "I, uh... We just met."

He raised his dark eyebrows. "So we did."

She shook her head. Why was he making her so unsettled? Good Heavens, she was usually more articulate than this! "I mean, you haven't interviewed me. Don't you want to know...more?"

He shrugged and inclined his head to one side. "Mademoiselle, I'm known for being a good judge of character, with very few exceptions. It's part of what has made me so successful. Jean-Philippe needs someone who is good with children, experienced and speaks French. From what I heard, you are all of these things."

Veronica felt a warm flush rising up her neck, straight to her cheeks then right on up to her hairline. For some reason, the idea of not being aware of *this* man, with his outsize presence, made her beyond flustered. "You were listening?" she asked in a voice that was, she congratulated herself, almost normal.

He shrugged in a wonderfully Mediterranean way. "Not on purpose, but the door was cracked open and sound carries down the hallway."

Mentally replaying her conversation with Jean-Philippe, Veronica couldn't figure out what she could possibly have said to warrant this instant acceptance. "And I said enough to give you such confidence?"

She thought she had gotten over her initial shock of awareness at how very handsome he was, like someone jumping into cold water who starts acclimating. She was wrong. When he turned the full force of his dark, soulful eyes on her and turned up the corners of his mouth in what might have been the beginnings of a smile, she nearly had to catch her breath. She felt the goosebumps rise again all over her arms.

"You did pass the background check with flying colors, and you must know your accent is beautiful. But mostly, you didn't miss a beat when my son insulted your er…ensemble." He motioned tactfully to her suit and she opened her mouth in indignation, only to snap it shut at his next words. "I truly believe you to be a young woman of good sense, patience and kindness. Those are qualities I value beyond all others."

His praise warmed her and was so close to describing the kind of person she hoped she was that she felt like another piece clicked into the odd connection she might be starting to feel with him.

"Thank you. In that case, I accept the position." He didn't return her smile, but she thought maybe his eyes crinkled the slightest bit at the corners.

"I'll have Monsieur Hormet bring in the paperwork. Come along, Jean-Phillipe," he said, turning and making his slow, deliberate way to the door with a gait she suspected concealed very-well-hidden pain. Jean-Philippe overtook him to sprint out of the door before his father.

All in all, Veronica was feeling pretty darn satisfied and relieved at avoiding the stress of a real interview when she heard Monsieur Reynard's last words before he left the room.

"Such a relief to meet a young woman who doesn't trouble herself too much over her clothes."

Chapter Two

As he gave her a sheaf of papers to review, Monsieur Hormet went over a few details, some of which she'd known and others that were new to her. Speaking succinctly, he told her that it was her new employer's desire that Jean-Philippe should speak English a majority of the time, but that he also wanted his son to feel comfortable speaking French with his au pair if the little boy felt like it. Jean-Philippe had apparently had a long-time nanny who had only recently retired, right after *the accident*. Monsieur Hormet said that in a hushed tone, almost as if he wished he didn't have to say it at all. Since then, one of the maids, Yvette, had been working extra, taking care of Jean-Philippe as well. The position was to begin immediately, if that were convenient for her. A little dazed by the veritable deluge of information, especially after so much secrecy, Veronica nodded her agreement. She didn't have anywhere else to be, after all.

After she'd read and signed the extensive paperwork, including even more detailed nondisclosure and confidentiality requirements that seemed a little excessive, even for a millionaire or billionaire—or whatever Monsieur Reynard was— Monsieur Hormet showed her to what would be her room. It was on the second floor, on the side facing the ocean, and the view was truly spectacular. The room itself was lovely as well, decorated with antique furnishings like an enormous mahogany bed, complete with a dark-blue satin coverlet. The dresser and wardrobe looked like something from a museum but also somehow well-loved. Everything was clean and well-kept, all the colors blues, creams and golds. Veronica's mind flashed to her bedroom back in her apartment in Boston and she grimaced at the comparison. She'd definitely left at least two discarded outfits strewn onto her floral bedspread, which didn't really match the rest of the colors of the room but that she loved anyway.

Before she could spend too long doing whatever 'freshening up' Monsieur Hormet expected her to do, she heard a door swing open on well-oiled hinges, and a golden-haired ball of energy ran into the room.

"Mademoiselle Carson, you're staying! I'm so excited! When are you going into town?"

Veronica smiled at the mix of French and English, all enthusiastic. "Please, you can call me Veronica, since I plan to call you Jean-Philippe?" she began. It took her another second—geez, she was getting rusty—until she puzzled out why he'd asked his question. "And you mean when am I going to bring you a surprise?"

Jean-Philippe nodded, smiling broadly and showing rows of even, white baby teeth.

She held out her hands. "I'm not certain exactly when, but I think it will be soon since I have to get more of my things. In the meantime, how about if we get to know each other? You can tell me what some of your favorite things are. You know, lots of activities that we do could be like a fun surprise."

The little boy nodded, clearly interested, and crept closer.

"I like to go to the beach. Papa says I can't go by myself, but sometimes, when he says he will take me, he has to work. Do you like seashells?"

Her mouth turning up in a smile, Veronica thought back to all the happy days she'd spent on the beach with her younger brothers, building sandcastles and decorating them with shell windows and doors. "Absolutely. Seashells are awesome. Did you know that they used to be homes for sea creatures?"

Jean-Philippe looked intrigued. "They're like skeletons?"

Veronica thought about it. "Well, sometimes I suppose they are. Like exoskeletons of some creatures — that means skeletons they wear on the outside instead of the inside. But other creatures move out of their shells when they get a new home, like hermit crabs, for instance. As they grow, they leave behind their old shell, which is getting too small." She imitated a crab crawling with her fingers over the bedspread, making a swishing sound on the satin. "Then they go, fast as they can, to find another shell that they think might fit better."

Jean-Philippe nodded sagely. "I get new clothes when my pants pop open when I sit down. We had to come to this house when the one where we lived burned down. Some people said the house was tracig…trajkig…tragic — but I liked it…and my friends. Louis had two poodles. Those are dogs, did you know?"

How could she ever have forgotten the candor of preschoolers? And what did he mean by 'tragic'? She was hardly going to ask Jean-Philippe for details, but she couldn't help but wonder. "I'm sorry. It sounds like you miss your home and your friends."

"Jean-Philippe, you were supposed to stay with Yvette until Mademoiselle Carson had a chance to settle in." The deep voice from the doorway made Veronica spring to her feet. As it had before, the sight of the tall form of the voice's owner made her heartbeat pound and her nerve endings tingle. Something about Monsieur Reynard drew her attention like no one else did. Perhaps like no one ever had.

"Mademoiselle Carson says I can call her Veronica, and she will call me Jean-Philippe," the little boy piped in.

"Is that correct? Sometimes Jean-Philippe...well, *often*...he has a great imagination." Monsieur Reynard turned to her as he spoke.

The sinking feeling in her stomach warned her that perhaps the household was set up somewhat more formally, but he was a little boy, for heaven's sake. She was hardly going to have a four-year-old calling her 'Mademoiselle Carson'. Veronica raised her chin.

"He understood me correctly. Actually, I hope everyone will call me Veronica. I don't think I've really ever been called Miss, or Mademoiselle, Carson." If she'd thought her new employer might have asked her to call him whatever his first name was in return, she would have been disappointed.

"Just so. I will let the rest of the staff know. And now, Jean-Philippe, I believe we've taken enough of, er, Veronica's time to relax and freshen up."

"I don't mind if he stays. I, um, don't really have much to unpack or...freshen." She felt her cheeks grow warm as she gestured lamely at the large briefcase where she'd shoved a quick change of clothes and two sets of underwear, in case the interview had gone late and she'd missed the last train.

He raised one dark eyebrow. "Indeed. I must apologize for not considering your plans with my impulsive offer. You would not have expected to be staying any length of time."

"Oh, no problem. I understand," she hurried to reassure him, and he quirked his lips in a wry smile.

"And I appreciate that, but the issue remains. If it is convenient, would you consider purchasing whatever you might need for the next week in the town here — at my expense, of course — then perhaps you could travel back to Boston with me next Wednesday for the day to pack your things? I'm afraid we'd have to leave quite early — I have an eleven o'clock meeting — but then you'd have the day and we'd be back by the evening."

At the idea of spending hours traveling in a car with this man going to and from Boston, a wave of something that could have been either excitement or panic swept over her. "Oh, that's not necessary… I can just —" Veronica wasn't sure how she had planned to finish that sentence, but Monsieur Reynard cut her off.

"No, no, I insist. You are now my employee, a valued member of my household. More, you will be guardian to all that I hold precious — Jean-Philippe, my heart itself."

His words and tone took her by surprise, so unexpectedly tender coming from someone who seemed otherwise formal and almost remote. But as he spoke, she heard the underlying truth in his voice. He loved his son fiercely.

"Of course. Thank you, then," she agreed.

"There are hours before it gets dark and we eat dinner. Maybe Veronica should go to town now?"

Monsieur Reynard looked at his son's smiling face curiously. "That's true. So it would be a fine time to go—"

"Yay!" Jean-Philippe cheered. Veronica's lips twitched as she held in her laughter, and her new employer looked at her questioningly.

"I believe he's recalling that I mentioned I would bring him a surprise the next time I went to town," she explained.

Monsieur Reynard didn't actually smile, but his eyes softened so that she felt suddenly warmer. "I see you've already learned about one of this little rascal's favorite things. There can never be too many surprises."

"He might have implied something like that," she answered, letting herself laugh openly. "And I'm happy to go now. I don't have any other plans, after all."

Oddly, her informal words seemed to cool the temperature of the room, and she wished she could recall them.

"Monsieur Hormet will take you, then, and I'll instruct him to have any of the clothing shops bill me directly. No need to be"—he paused, as if searching for a tactful word—"overly practical," he finally settled on. "You can choose something both sensible and becoming without worrying over the cost."

Is my choice of jacket today going to haunt my nightmares? Veronica wondered. She didn't usually dress like that but it had been an *interview! Good Lord.* Didn't anyone in this household know that someone was dressing to please any audience in a job interview?

"Thank you. I'll do my best," she answered tartly. She thought he'd missed the hint of sarcasm, but as she passed him after he'd motioned her ahead of him, she caught what might have been a gleam of amusement in his eyes. Perhaps Monsieur Reynard wasn't made of marble after all.

As Alain left the room, he realized what the unfamiliar sensation was in his chest. Lightness. Humor. He thought he might actually *like* the somewhat-plain young woman. Veronica. The name didn't seem to suit her, but he liked how she'd insisted everyone call her that, although he had noticed that she'd realized it was an unusual request.

His gut sense—and he'd built his vast business empire in large part on his sense about people—told him that he couldn't have found a better companion for his little boy. And while his impulsively revealing words had surprised him as well as the young lady, nothing could have been truer. Jean-Philippe was the center of his world. The lightness and joy his son brought with him illuminated even the darkest parts of Alain's sorrow and grief.

Whereas before the recent events at their home in Nice, he had sometimes taken his child's continued safety and presence for granted, now everything he did was for Jean-Philippe. He'd moved a greatly reduced portion of their household to their smallest and remotest home here in Maine, partly to keep himself away from the relentless press but mostly for his son—to ensure that Jean-Philippe could run free and enjoy himself without the constant scrutiny of the media and the speculation and suspicion, along with the constant vicious gossip that they couldn't escape in any reach of French society.

The irony of his choice of location wasn't lost on him, though. This was one of the homes he'd inherited from his father, and his father had had the historic castle moved by boat, brick by brick, from Northern France as a grand romantic gesture to his American wife. It had always been their special place and idyllic for Alain and his brother, Marius, when they'd visited during some of their childhood summer vacations. After his parents had passed away, Alain, too, had shared it with his wife, Joëlle, when they'd been newlyweds. He'd once thought it could become their special place as well, but of course he'd been wrong in the end, as he'd been wrong about so many things related to Joëlle. They'd never brought Jean-Philippe to visit. Alain hadn't had time for long vacations. Or, really, he hadn't made time. But now, making time for his son, considering his son's wants and needs, was the most important thing to him.

Sometimes, in the past couple of weeks since they'd arrived, he thought he might even have felt the spirits of those who were gone. Fanciful, but he'd imagined he'd smelled his mother's perfume or the flowers he and his brother would pick for her from the edge of the forest nearby.

He could have sworn he'd heard his wife's silvery laughter, too. He'd been drawn to so many things about Joëlle when they'd met, but her laughter, the way her lovely face would light up with happiness, was something he'd never forget. It had lost that later, but her laughter was something he'd seen often when they'd come here together. This castle felt almost haunted, not with sadness but with memories that were now sad all the same. He hoped that Jean-Philippe and his new au pair could chase those memories away with new ones…better ones.

Shaking off his melancholy thoughts — and since when had he become so maudlin? — Alain continued to his office. His steps were still painful, especially if he'd walked a lot on any given day, but he could now mostly hide his grimaces and stiffness if he walked very slowly. Deliberately. He'd definitely walked too much today, though, and he would have to put his leg up when he sat down. Just before he went into his office, intent on doing one last videoconference call with a major Parisian client before it got too late in Europe, he couldn't help but smile, and the sensation of using those facial muscles was unfamiliar.

He hadn't missed the way Veronica's eyes had flashed and her chest had heaved indignantly, even though she'd tried to hide it, at his suggestion that she not be too frugal in her choices. Plain she might be, but underneath it there was some fire as well. He genuinely hoped she had some fun shopping in town, and he already wondered what she would bring back for Jean-Philippe, curious in spite of himself. He felt a strange quickening in his pulse as he thought of her generous curves, how soft she looked like she would be if he touched her, kissed her, held her against his body. Then he put all thoughts of her out of his head and focused on business.

Chapter Three

Grant's Cliff was only a couple of miles at most from the castle, and the town was surprisingly large, but several of the cafes and gift shops along the center of the main street downtown were still closed for the season. Contrary to what the conductor had said, it looked like a tourist destination after all—but a small one. Veronica had been to Camden once on a long-ago summer daytrip, and to several towns in Southern Maine, but Grant's Cliff felt more...authentic somehow, like it was as much for locals as for tourists. Since another name for Maine was 'Vacationland'— heck, it was even on the license plates—she thought this was possibly unusual for a coastal town. There were a number of boutiques to choose from, but she worried both that they weren't really her style, and that the clothes they sold also weren't entirely appropriate attire for running after a four-year-old all day. With relief, she spotted a tiny department store right at the edge of the downtown area—like, the smallest version of a department store that she had ever seen. Still, she recognized the name and knew it would have everything.

Monsieur Hormet followed her inside after helping her out of the car, and she felt a bit like a celebrity with a very small entourage. Everyone—well, all five or so of the other customers—turned to look at her, and she blushed before going toward the women's clothing section. At first, she was sparing in what she picked up, but then, recalling Monsieur Reynard's instruction not to be overly conservative, she added several extra knit tops and sweaters, along with practical pants, to her pile. When she got to socks, underwear and nightgowns, Monsieur Hormet cleared his throat and looked pointedly elsewhere, which made her smile. She could have sworn a dull flush colored his weathered cheeks, too.

She hauled all her selections to the dressing room, with the help of a salesclerk who must have been all of seventeen years old, and started to try on the first outfit. As she tugged on the fleece-lined jeans and sweater, she realized she wasn't alone.

"...*dangerous up there. I won't even let Caitlin and Connor play there anymore, since the beast is back.*"

She couldn't make out every word of the women's hushed conversation, but her ears practically burned when she heard someone else mention the beast. *What the heck?*

"...*not safe...should be illegal...that little boy.*" The other woman's voice was even lower, but her words were more urgent.

When Veronica heard the doors next to her open, she hurried to finish pulling on her sweater, but she was too late to see anything more than the retreating backs of two women walking down the narrow center aisle of the women's department. What had they meant? From what they'd said, it sounded more like they were talking about a person than an animal, but who would call a person a beast? And why? Would she and Jean-Philippe be unsafe on the day trips she was already mentally planning for them?

The teenaged clerk was waiting for her, and the girl's genuine enthusiasm for Veronica's choices soon made her forget the odd conversation. She ended up buying a new outfit for every day of the week — she'd show him she didn't have to be overly practical! — along with enough underthings as well. She felt kind of bad for buying a pair of ultra-sensible waterproof hiking boots, because she actually hadn't owned that type of shoe since she'd been a kid. Also, she was reasonably certain Monsieur Reynard would be appalled at anyone owning something so utterly functional. In fact, she tried to pay for the boots herself, but everything had already been put together on one tab. She decided she would pay Monsieur Reynard back and explain the error, since she was going to have to buy something like those boots for the new job anyway. At the last minute, she also added a dress, since she wasn't really sure what every part of her job would be. The lifestyle of the château just wasn't something she could guess at, and she wanted to be prepared — and to avoid ever wearing her interview suit again if possible.

She smiled to herself as they were leaving until she realized that everyone looked at her again. Studied her, actually. She gave a vague smile to the store at large and reasoned that they must not get a lot of visitors this time of year. Still, it was weird.

After they'd put the bags into the car, she stopped Monsieur Hormet before they got back in. "Is there a candy or toy shop?"

The twinkle in his eyes told her he knew why she was asking. "There are several, but most are still closed for the season. There's a nice little souvenir shop that sells silly things and sweets over there." He motioned to the next block. When he would have followed her, she waved him away.

"No, no…you stay here. I'll only be five minutes." The air was still cool, but some sun must have broken through the earlier gloom at last, and she loved how fresh it made everything feel. She could see and hear the ocean from almost everywhere in the small downtown, too. It felt like a really quaint New England fishing village with high-end touches.

The souvenir shop was filled to the brim with all sorts of things, and she could see it would be a little boy's paradise. It had everything from wind-up lobsters to bulk candy and fudge, along with sunglasses and T-shirts and all the usual stuff. As she walked in, there was a woman talking to the store clerk, but conversation halted as soon as the bell over the door rang, announcing her presence. Still, she thought she'd heard *'working for the beast.'*

"Hello," she ventured, using her friendliest tone.

The two women smiled but didn't respond.

Mindful of Monsieur Hormet waiting, she made a quick circuit of the store and was happy to find a little plastic sea-creature set. She thought Jean-Philippe would love it, and it would be something portable for them to play with on a daytrip and to make up stories about. At the register, she grabbed a couple of pieces of locally-made salt-water taffy too, just because, well…*yum*. She thought she might have to eat one on the way home. The clerk rang her up in near-silence, while the other shopper stood to one side, and she could feel their eyes as they both watched her leave.

Veronica fought the urge to brush her back to be sure something wasn't stuck there. She'd thought Maineiacs were supposed to be friendlier than Bostonians, who could be a bit surly, but wow. What was with this town?

Monsieur Hormet's face creased into a smile when he saw what she had bought.

"Excellent choice, Mademoiselle," he said, opening the door for her to slide in.

"Thanks, and I hope you'll call me Veronica. Monsieur Reynard said he'd let everyone know, but there probably hasn't been time—"

"Of course, Mademoiselle Veronica. With pleasure," Monsieur Hormet answered, and she had to hide her smile. Well, at least he was calling her Veronica…sort of.

After the short ride back to the castle, he insisted on taking her bags to her room.

"You have a little time, Mademoiselle Veronica. Monsieur Reynard and Jean-Philippe won't be expecting you for dinner until six-thirty. Yvette will probably be giving Jean-Philippe his bath, in fact."

Veronica looked out again at the spectacular view, then smiled broadly back at Monsieur Hormet. "Thank you…then I think I'll stay out her for a little while longer, to take a quick walk, if that's all right?"

The older man nodded. "Of course. All this land— practically everything you can see, in fact—belongs to the Reynards, so you can go anywhere without trespassing. There's a path to a little beach." He gestured toward what she saw was a break in the rocks a quarter mile to her right. "It's an easy hike down and very beautiful, although the water can be too rough for swimming. Not that it's warm enough to consider that today anyway."

"*Merci encore*, Monsieur Hormet," Veronica answered, already starting off in that direction. The older man seemed just lovely, even if his manner was little austere.

The pale sun was setting, and in spite of the remaining gray clouds that formed billowing mounds in the sky, there were hints of glorious red, orange and pink, with a bit of violet mixed in as well. She stopped near the edge of the rocky cliffs and took a deep breath, startled when she felt her phone buzz in her pocket.

She looked down to see she'd missed four text messages from Katrin.

How'd it go?

Knew it… You must have gotten the job! Congrats!

Okay. Not stalking you but now it's been a while. No reception??

The last one, just sent, made her nearly laugh out loud.

If I don't hear from you in the next ten minutes, I'm assuming you're chained up in a dungeon with only moldy bread crust and dirty water to sustain you, several rats your only friends and companions and I'll be forced to call your brother and stage a covert rescue operation.

She typed her reply.

Sorry! Got the job, starting right away, so went to town for more clothes. Reception a little spotty here, but okay right at the house.

She smiled and typed a second message.

You were right. Very Gothic. :)

Mindful of all the paperwork she'd signed and also the general sense she got that Monsieur Reynard was very private, she avoided the house and snapped some pictures of the view with her cell phone, then turned and pressed the flip button on her camera to take a selfie of herself with the ocean behind her. She'd taken a couple, one of which didn't make her look too awful, although her hair was flying every which way, and started to type a message to go with it when her phone was snatched from her hand.

Monsieur Reynard was angry—furious, even—so that his eyes were thunderous and every line of his tall frame was taut with barely leashed rage.

"Who are you working for? Who sent you?" he demanded.

"*What*? I'm working for you—or I thought I was. Madame Montreaux recommended me." Veronica was genuinely confused and a little freaked out, but she tried to be patient. Maybe something had happened to damage his memory in his recent accident? Still, the look he was giving her sent a chill down her spine. In spite of his injuries, this was a powerful, dangerous man—especially now, when the usually-charming façade was down.

"Yeah, sure. What newspaper? Website? Who are you sending pictures to?" He barked out the questions, stepping closer—so close that Veronica could smell his spicy cologne and feel the heat radiating off of him. And how the heck had he gotten down here from the house so fast?

Her mouth fell open. "I'm not working for anyone. I was just sending pictures to my friend. You can read them," she offered, then added with a snap, "although I don't appreciate your taking my phone from me."

He glanced at the partially typed message. "Proof of life?" He raised his eyebrow.

"It's…ah, an inside joke," she explained.

He scrolled up and she swore he nearly smiled in spite of himself. "Locked in a dungeon, eh?"

She grabbed her phone back. "You weren't supposed to see that." She closed the messages and opened the pictures.

"Here." She handed him back the phone to show the photos she'd just taken. "They're all just the ocean. I didn't think you'd appreciate me taking pictures of the house."

Monsieur Reynard looked through them, the last of the tension draining from his frame. "It would appear I owe you a very sincere apology. I, ah, have no excuse except that the French press has been relentless since the…accident, and I thought…. When I saw you taking pictures, I assumed they'd managed to even reach us here. I just want to protect Jean-Philippe."

Veronica considered what he'd said. His apology had seemed honest, and he looked contrite. She didn't think he was a man who was accustomed to being wrong, but she appreciated that he'd admitted it right away. Now that the tense moment had passed, she noticed how close they were standing to each other. Alone. It felt curiously intimate, and he must have sensed it too, since he took an awkward step backward.

"Apology accepted," she finally answered. "I hope you don't take this the wrong way, but I really don't know who you and Jean-Philippe are, other than family friends of Madame Montreaux—or at least that was the vague impression I got from her. However, I can't imagine going through something so...difficult, then having to deal with it being publicized on top of that."

He grimaced. "I think that's a good reminder that perhaps I'm not as famous as I think I am."

She smiled at his self-deprecating tone. "Well, don't feel too bad. I don't usually have time to read *People*, much less *Paris Match*." She named one of the most famous magazines in France. "I once saw a Hollywood actor in a coffee shop and asked him if we'd gone to college together."

His answering huff of laughter was as sudden as it was surprising, and it sounded rusty, like he didn't laugh very often.

"What did he say?"

She bit her lip. "He just said that no, we hadn't." She laughed at the memory. "I wouldn't know who he was even now, except a couple of people came up to him asking for autographs right afterward. I was mortified."

He started to hand her phone back, pushing the button to go back to her home screen, but he stopped when he glanced at the screensaver picture that had popped up. Veronica's breath caught in her throat. It was a picture of her on the beach, flanked by two tall, handsome young men. It had been breezy that day, so their hair was all windblown, and the smiles on their faces were broad and utterly carefree. It was what she thought of as 'The Last Best Day'.

She willed him not to ask about it and something must have shone in her eyes, since he just handed the phone back to her without comment.

"I'll see you for dinner?" He made it a question.

"Definitely. See you soon. Actually, I'd better go get ready," she answered, turning back toward the house.

"Of course," he answered in a bored tone, and she recognized it for the dismissal he'd meant it to be. Monsieur Reynard was a study in contradictions, it seemed, but now she'd seen beneath his charming and remote persona to the real man. She'd thought him attractive before, mysterious, but now...*now* she realized he might be dangerous. Oh, she didn't think he would harm anyone, though she would never like to be on the receiving end of his wrath, that was for sure. No, he was dangerous to her peace of mind. She found him unsettling, but try as she might, she couldn't stop thinking about him and his unwilling laughter, the heat of his body close to hers. And now she was going to be living in his household.

She was going to have to be careful.

Chapter Four

Waiting in the little salon for his son and Mademoiselle…no, Veronica, he would call her Veronica. The informality of it suited her. Waiting for the two of them to arrive, Alain poured himself a small *pastis* from the tray on top of the liquor cabinet. Hormet knew him well and had left a small pitcher of iced water as well to combine with the *pastis* until it turned the perfect shade of opaque light yellow. The licorice smell of *pastis* always reminded him of his father's family, who were from the south of France. Provence. Warm, wholesome, and kind, they'd loved their children and grandchildren. And his grandfather had always given them anise-flavored treats.

He'd surprised himself by making such a blunder with Veronica today about the photos on her phone. It was unlike him to be so wrong about someone's intentions, but then, he reminded himself, he'd been wrong a couple of other times recently too. *Spectacularly wrong*. In fact, for someone who'd built his entire business, his entire fortune, on being such a shrewd judge of character, he was having quite a rough patch lately.

His laughter was humorless. Even in his own thoughts, he was downplaying the enormity of what had gone wrong. He supposed he didn't want to face it, even in his own mind. Because then he might have to be honest with himself, and he just wasn't sure he was ready for that. Not yet, anyway.

He was saved from the grim turn of his thoughts by his son's happy chatter as the little boy burst into the room.

"Papa! Veronica brought me sea creatures. Lots of them. There's a stingray and a manta ray and a giant squid and an orca! Look!" He held some sort of plastic toy as high up as he could reach, which was just about to his father's chest, given how tall Alain was, but Jean-Philippe valiantly stood on his very tiptoes.

"Amazing!" Alain answered, studying the plastic figure as though it were a work of art in a museum. "That looks just like the orca we saw on the whale-watch last summer in Alaska, don't you think?"

Jean-Philippe nodded excitedly as Veronica followed him into the room, the skirt of her simple new dress swishing against the doorframe.

"I love orcas. They're predators. Killer whales. Sea wolves. Sometimes they eat sharks. That's cool! Papa and I saw a whole pod last summer, didn't we? I think this looks like the mama orca…or maybe the baby. Orcas are really large. But blue whales are bigger."

Alain tried to stop himself, but he couldn't help but look to see what her reaction was to his son's excited monologue. He was accustomed to it, but to an outsider, it might be daunting. Or, as it had been for Jean-Philippe's mother, boring.

Their eyes met over Jean-Philippe's blond head, and their gazes locked. Her eyes were gray — how had he not noticed their unusual color before? — and deeply amused, not in a condescending way, though. He could tell that immediately. No, Veronica liked his son. She was listening to the child, really listening, in spite of the rapid-fire stream of consciousness that Jean-Philippe often spoke in. The look she gave to Alain warmed him and also made him feel guilty. The warmth was from the connection they shared in that moment, the amusement and appreciation they felt over Jean-Philippe's unadulterated enthusiasm.

But for Alain, the guilt followed just as surely, since his wife, Joëlle, would never hear this. In fact, she'd never liked hearing it when she'd had the chance. She'd found having Jean-Philippe to be deeply inconvenient, and while she had liked dressing him up, she'd never really grown to like him as a person in his own right. If she were here instead of the new au pair, she wouldn't have been able to get away fast enough. But he still felt guilty, nonetheless.

He cleared his throat to hide his discomfort. "Would you like a drink, Madam — er, Veronica?"

She hesitated, and he could almost see the thoughts in her head since her face was so open. She wasn't sure what the right answer was. She was clearly weighing if should she refuse because she was new…or was it more polite to accept something?

"Perhaps a small sherry or port? I'm having *pastis*, if that's something you enjoy." He didn't know why he made the suggestion, except that he didn't like seeing her uncomfortable for some reason. Also, her dress wasn't nearly as plain as he'd thought, but instead seemed to hug her curves lovingly in a most distracting way.

Jean-Philippe's voice broke the spell of his contemplation of her dress. "I'd like seltzer with lime, please, Papa," his son said, in between moving his toy around and making orca noises. Really high-pitched ones. They were actually pretty spot on, Alain noted with pride, even though his eardrums might not thank him.

"Of course, *mon grand*," Alain answered, smiling down at his little boy while he jokingly called him the French equivalent of 'big guy'.

"I would love a *pastis*, then. Thank you." Her tone was cautious and a little prim, and for some reason she made him want to smile yet again. He raised both eyebrows at her choice. He could come to love that snippy tone of voice, and the lush way she pursed her lips.

"*Pastis*? Have you had it before, then?"

A curious expression, a mixture of both absolute love and deep sorrow, crossed her face. It was only there for a second, but it was unmistakable. Alain recognized it. And he realized it was the same expression she'd worn when she'd looked at the picture — the little screensaver — on her phone.

"Yes, just a few times, but I liked it. I studied in Paris for a semester when I was in college but took a trip once to the South, near Aix-en-Provence."

Tamping down his curiosity, Alain deftly prepared both Veronica's and Jean-Philippe's drinks. Their fingers brushed, only for an instant, as he handed her glass to her. In spite of the icy glass, he felt a warm shock travel from where their fingertips met all the way through his body. He drew his hand back as if burned, and she did something similar, splashing liquid onto her dress. He didn't meet her eyes as he ruthlessly tried to bring the evening back to a more social footing. Polite. Distant.

"Aix is beautiful...near where my father's family is from." He'd tried for some of the charming small talk his peers excelled at, but instead, he'd revealed more of himself. Why had he chosen those words? He almost never spoke of his father's family anymore. He was deeply uncomfortable with how much he feared he was already growing to like her, and he took a mental step back.

Unconscious of his blunder, Veronica answered politely, "Oh, yes. Such gorgeous architecture. I never knew the Romans had really lived there so much, built so many buildings. But I didn't like the arenas." Her eyes softened with compassion. "It's almost as though you could feel all the battles that must have happened there." She stopped short of saying the word, probably out of deference to Jean-Philippe, but Alain knew exactly what she meant. All the death... He'd felt it, too. Someone always didn't come away from a battle, and often neither side survived. It was an insightful comment, but it showed him how sensitive she was. The last thing someone should be around him was sensitive.

He cleared his throat to answer, but Jean-Philippe spoke again first.

"My *maman* was in an accident. With Sébastien, too. I liked him. He brought me sweets. But I like sea creatures more than sweets."

Alain knew the comment was innocent. *Mon Dieu*, Jean-Philippe was innocent in every way, but it stirred a fire that he kept carefully banked—a fire that, despite all of his efforts, was just waiting to flare to life at any moment — anger, raw and primal. Sébastien had been his closest friend, his closest business partner and a frequent visitor to their home. Then he'd utterly betrayed Alain in every way — and Joëlle…

Just like that, there wasn't enough air in the room, and Alain needed to breathe. More, he needed to get away from Jean-Philippe to keep him innocent, oblivious to the truth for as long as possible. Oddly, he wanted to protect the new au pair as well. Veronica, with her air of patience and goodness, even if he could sense she'd seen some sadness in her past.

He set down his drink and pointedly looked at his watch. "I'm sorry. I had forgotten a call I have to make before the markets open in Hong Kong," he said, and his tone was flat, his words sounding hollow, even to his own ears. He had to get out of the house, into the cool night air. "Forgive me. Another evening. Enjoy your supper."

Without really looking at Veronica, he could tell she was taken aback. Jean-Philippe looked disappointed, too, but he handled it better because, to Alain's shame, his son had had a lot of practice.

The bitter aftertaste of his carefully modulated lie still on his tongue, he turned without another word and walked with deliberate care out of the room, continuing straight out of the front door into the dark evening mist.

After Monsieur Reynard's abrupt departure, Veronica looked down at Jean-Philippe. His face was downcast but stoic. It made her heart hurt. Clearly, this had happened before — which was odd, since it had been obvious to her earlier, several times already, that Monsieur Reynard adored his little son. But she guessed he was probably a workaholic, too. No one got to be a mega-millionaire by keeping a good work-life balance. She was still learning the layout of the house after her brief tour earlier. When he'd left, he hadn't looked like he was headed toward the wing with his office area, but she supposed he could have multiple workspaces.

Shaking off her musings, she smiled brightly for Jean-Philippe's benefit. "Since it's just us, do we get extra dessert?" she asked, and he brightened immediately.

"Do we?" he asked.

She shrugged, taking a last sip of her drink. "I'm not sure, but I am definitely going to eat all my meat and vegetables so I can find out."

Jean-Philippe nodded. "Me too," he answered, echoing her enthusiastic tone, and they went into the dining room.

It seemed a little silly to have such a fancy layout for two people, especially since those two people were an au pair and a four-year-old, but Monsieur Hormet's face as he served them was absolutely impassive. Veronica was jealous, actually. She'd always wanted to possess the skill of not wearing her every thought on her face, but she'd never learned the art. She made a mental note as they were eating salad to ask him later.

Dinner was delicious, and very, very French. Cassoulet with salad to follow, then a cheese course, finished with a crème brulée. Her favorite. It was no hardship to agree to share a second helping of dessert with Jean-Philippe, although she was going to have to be careful if they really ate like this every night. Jean-Philippe's manners were excellent — way better than any other four-year-old she'd met before — but she reasoned that this was probably a much more normal part of his life than it would have been for her or her brothers at the same age. She marveled at how often he said 'please' and 'thank you', his formal posture and how he didn't bat an eyelash at sheep's milk cheese or a full salad. In fact, she thought she might need to step her own manners up a notch.

When they'd finished licking every last delicious drop of the creamy custard from their silver dessert spoons and no one had come to say anything about Jean-Philippe or his schedule, she decided she was going to have to wing it for the rest of the night. She lifted her chin, secretly pleased at the chance to show how well she was going to fit in.

"I heard you already had a bath. Is that right?" she asked.

Jean-Philippe nodded, making his blond curls bounce. "Yes, next it's story time! In my bed, but I don't have to go to sleep. Sometimes I close my eyes, but I don't have to." She could hear from the stubborn undertone that bedtime was probably a dirty word, but it was encouraging that he liked the rest of the nightly routine, at least.

"Then story time it is! And I bet you have a great bedroom, too." She smiled as they passed Monsieur Hormet, and she thought she saw approbation on his face.

Jean-Philippe told her all about his awesome room on the way upstairs, which she realized was just kitty-corner across the hall from her own. *Handy*. Her heart did a little clutching-clenching thing when he put his chubby little-boy hand into hers with absolute trust, and she recognized what might not be obvious during the day when he was running around like a crazy person. He was still just a baby, too.

The decorations in his room were a wild combination of animals, sea creatures, planets and dinosaurs, but everything looked clean and comfortable. She had to hide a smile when she thought of the look that must have been on some poor interior-decorator's face when he or she heard what the plans for this room were, especially given how tasteful and elegant most of the rest of the château seemed to be. Every corner was brimming with children's treasures and toys—and shelves of books as well. There was a play table, an eating table, an easel, a chalkboard and even a fake kitchen that looked practically big enough to prepare real meals in. Holy cow! Jean-Philippe had a child's dream bedroom, but his individual preferences were stamped onto it unmistakably as well.

His bed, which was a traditional and large four-poster bed in dark wood, with a comfortable chair drawn up next to it—*maybe by Yvette?*—was covered with a thick-looking duvet in plain black, and it was practically the only plain thing in the room. Folded on top of the covers were some pajamas made from fabric covered in rocket ships, and on the floor there were even little dinosaur slippers laid out. Jean-Philippe went right away to change into the pajamas, then he showed her the adjoining bathroom where he had his toothbrush and toothpaste. Both were dinosaur-themed.

He looked up at her suspiciously before he started to brush his teeth. "Nanny Marie used to let me choose for story time, but since she left, Yvette usually says she doesn't have time."

Veronica had to smile again. Working in a professional environment for the past couple of years had made her forget just how entertaining kids Jean-Philippe's age could be.

"I promise we'll have time for a story," she assured him, and he brushed his teeth with vigor as she watched with a critical eye to be sure he looked like he was getting everywhere in his mouth.

"So, what kind of a story do you want?" Veronica asked when he'd finished. "I think I can make up pretty much any kind, although I warn you, my dinosaur name pronunciations are imperfect, so you may have to correct me."

Jean-Philippe's eyes went wide and he looked impressed. "You tell your own stories? Nanny Marie had me choose books."

"You can choose two books, if you want."

He shook his head emphatically. "Oh no, I want a made-up story. Just for *me*!" His blue eyes sparkled and he practically danced on his toes with excitement.

Veronica hadn't intended to do anything that was so different or to get him extra excited right before bed, but she gave a mental shrug. Having her there was different, and he was bound to be a little extra excited tonight anyway.

"All right, then you get under the covers and tell me what stories you like best. Astronauts, dinosaurs, sea creatures, fairy tales—"

Settling into the giant bed, Jean-Philippe broke in. "Fairy tales! Yes, I *love* fairy tales."

Veronica sat down in the convenient chair. "Perfect. I love them, too." A little laugh escaped her as her little charge looked up at her expectantly. He looked positively dwarfed, such a young child in an enormous bed.

"Once upon a time—" she started.

"What does that mean?" Jean-Philippe interrupted. His English was so good that it was easy to forget that he was still learning.

"Oh, it's how most fairy tales begin. Like '*Il était une fois…*'"

He nodded knowledgeably. "Ah, okay then."

Hiding her smile at his magnanimous tone—she was going to have to watch his attitude—she started again.

"Once upon a time, there was a beast who lived alone in a castle."

"I know this one already!" Jean-Philippe complained, but Veronica shook her finger then tapped her ear gently.

"Listen. You may know a story about a beast, but this one is different."

He looked like he wanted to argue, but he stayed quiet.

"The beast was scary-looking and sounded ferocious. His growls were so loud they echoed off the mountains and hills. All the villagers were afraid of him."

Jean-Philippe's eyes grew wide. "Did he have big teeth?"

She nodded emphatically. "The biggest! Like steak knives, long and wickedly sharp. They even cut the beast's own lips sometimes, which made him sound even more terrible. You see, what the villagers didn't know was that the beast wasn't dangerous, but instead he was sad. None of the villagers knew it, that is, except one little boy. Ludo. Ludo fell down when he was out picking berries one afternoon and hurt his ankle. He'd gone farther away from home than he was supposed to." When Veronica paused, Jean-Philippe seemed to be listening avidly. "His foot got stuck under a tree root in a gully—"

"What's a gully?" Jean-Philippe asked.

"It's another word for a ditch, like a small valley."

He nodded and Veronica continued, but she noticed his eyes were beginning to look tired and his eyelids had started to droop, even as he was clearly fighting his fatigue.

"Well, Ludo's family and friends were out looking for him, calling for him, and looking in every cave and hole they could find, but they weren't looking far away in the woods near the beast's castle and so he was still stuck in the gully when it started to get dark. He was cold and hungry, and his ankle really hurt, so he started to cry. And that was how the beast heard him and found him."

When she stopped talking, Jean-Philippe's eyes, which had been closed, popped open immediately.

"Don't stop! I want to know what happened to Ludo!" he protested.

"I'm glad you liked it, *mon petit*, but it's getting late now. How about I tell you more tomorrow?"

"*Promettez?*" he asked, using the French word to ask her if she promised as he spoke sleepily.

"I promise," she agreed, and sat next to him for a moment longer until she was sure he was asleep, his cheeks flushed pink and his chest moving evenly up and down under his black bedspread. To her surprise, she felt more at peace than she had in a long time.

Chapter Five

Veronica woke slowly, savoring the feeling of the sumptuous bedding and the bed itself. It was more comfortable than anything she'd ever slept on before, hands down—better even than the fancy hotel where she'd had to stay once for an important conference she'd accompanied her former boss to, back before the company had gone bankrupt, partly due to over-spending. She'd thought *that* was luxury. She'd had no idea. Monsieur Reynard knew how to live. At the thought of her new boss, her heart sped up. She could imagine that he probably knew how to do all sorts of wonderful things.

Even as she luxuriated, happily ensconced in the dreamy state between sleep and wakefulness, she had an uncomfortable feeling, almost as if she were being watched. When she'd convinced herself that she was being overly imaginative, especially after all the rumors and the story she'd told Jean-Philippe the night before, she opened her eyes and shrieked at the face right next to hers.

She shot upright in bed, narrowly missing the face that was inches from her own which, when she was sitting, seemed curiously low. In the dim early-morning light of dawn, she could make out the features more clearly. Her breathing slowed and she felt a hysterical bubble of laughter roll right out her.

"Jean-Philippe! Oh my gosh, you scared me!"

"It's morning time. I can see blue in the sky, and that means I can get up. What are we going to do today?" He clambered onto the bed and stayed very close to her, with a complete and utter lack of understanding of personal space. "I'm e'cited."

She collapsed back onto the pillows, helpless with laughter. She'd honestly thought she was smack dab in the middle of a horror movie, trapped in a room with one of those freaky ghost children. Instead, it was an overly enthusiastic four-year-old. Or, rather, a four-year-old of normal enthusism, which was extremely high since he was only four.

"Why are you laughing?" He grinned, suddenly pleased with himself. "Am I funny?"

She ruffled his hair. "You are definitely funny. A regular little silly-billy."

He tilted his head to one side. "What's a silly-billy?" He pronounced it with an accent, so it sounded like *sillee billee*.

"Well, someone funny and fun, who does silly things."

He looked pleased again. "Thank you."

She had to laugh at how proud he seemed. "As for what we're going to do? You're going to go brush your teeth and wash your face, and I will do the same. I'll get dressed and meet you in your room so we can go down and have breakfast. Then we'll see about the rest of the day."

He slid down obediently. "Are we going to go on an adventure?"

Veronica folded her blanket back and hopped down as well, wishing she had slippers like Jean-Philippe's. The floors of the château were *cold*...icy, even. Or at least they felt like it to her toes, even through her socks. "A mini-adventure, absolutely!"

He whooped with excitement and scampered off, leaving her bemused.

She got ready and dressed in record time, pulling on one of the new casual outfits, thankful that she'd taken all of the tags off before going to sleep the night before. She wasn't sure how much Jean-Philippe could do for himself and how much he usually had help with. With visions of him eating a mound of toothpaste making her stomach twist with anxiety, she was relieved when she found him finishing up what looked like a normal morning hygiene routine in his bathroom on his own. His hair was pretty wet, with damp tendrils clinging all around his face, but at least he looked clean. She helped him put on an outfit that he'd chosen. He'd seemed surprised to be given a choice but had finally settled on a sweater with a moose on it and thick canvas pants — then they started downstairs. When she would have turned back toward the dining room, he tugged her hand in another direction, laughing.

"Not that way! Did you think we eat *breakfast* in the *dining* room?" Jean-Philippe chuckled as if she'd made a joke, and Veronica felt a bit out of her league. "We eat breakfast in the *breakfast* room, silly-billy!"

His logic was unimpeachable, if someone knew there were both a dining room and a breakfast room, and Veronica couldn't be mad, but she did have a flash of worry about how many more things like this she just wasn't going to be able to guess.

As they entered the room which must be the breakfast room, something changed in the air—some scent or feeling, maybe the actual molecules of the room vibrated differently—and she knew without even looking up who she would find there. And there he was, sitting at the head of the big wooden table, sipping from a large cup of coffee. *Café au lait*, she would guess. Alain Reynard—she had finally learned his first name from an envelope on what looked like a tray of correspondence just outside the door to the breakfast room—looked as handsome and powerful as he had the night before, but she noticed there were small lines of strain around his mouth, as if maybe he hadn't slept well.

"*Bonjour...* Good morning," he greeted them a little absently over the morning edition of a financial newspaper, rising to his feet slowly and with a somewhat-distracted air.

Jean-Philippe rushed over to his father, who bent over so his son could kiss him on both cheeks—wet, smacking kisses.

"Good morning," Veronica answered, feeling suddenly shy. For some reason, she'd expected that she and Jean-Philippe would be on their own for most of the day and the morning meal, but of course, Alain lived here too. It was his house, after all. She decided to give in to the wicked impulse to mentally call him Alain, even though she knew she'd have to be careful not to slip up and call him anything but Monsieur

Reynard out loud. Even the thought of the intimacy of using his name in her thoughts gave her a frisson of excitement, and she chided herself for being so susceptible to everything about him.

"Aren't you going to *fais la bise* with Veronica, Papa?" Jean-Philippe asked, his blond curls bouncing as he trained his head from his father to his au pair. Veronica recognized that he referred to the French custom of kissing every time you saw someone for the first time in a day — or said goodbye or goodnight.

She felt her cheeks heat up as Alain caught her gaze, which was silly. She'd studied at a Parisian university and her French classmates had kissed her every day. Their parents had kissed her when they'd met her. It was crazy to feel her heartbeat quicken at the idea of being kissed by Alain in what for him would be a totally commonplace gesture.

As if he could feel her discomfort, Alain spoke to his young son.

"*Mon petit chou*, not everyone greets each other the way we do. In fact, in the United States, a handshake or hug, depending on how close you are — or even nothing at all — is most common," he explained.

Jean-Philippe gaped in astonishment at his father's words. "But why? That doesn't make sense. And besides, Veronica understands French. Right?" He turned big blue eyes on Veronica that begged her to agree.

Alain's look was inscrutable as he spoke to her. "I'm sorry. We've really continued to keep a totally French household, so Jean-Philippe hasn't felt like things have changed much from one home to another, but…there are certain inconsistencies between us and American societal norms."

Veronica shook her head, feeling bad that this was becoming such a big thing, when really, it was a very normal part of daily French life. It was certainly of no consequence to Alain, so why should it be to her? "Not a problem. I, ah…don't mind." She felt her cheeks burn hotter as she realized how that had sounded, so she hastened to explain. "I mean, I got used to being kissed when I was studying in Paris."

Alain raised one dark eyebrow. He didn't smile, but his eyes were amused. "Indeed?"

"Not…like that. It's just that all my friends—older men, younger men, everyone—kissed me," she stammered. "Women too, of course."

Now Alain's lips twitched, and Veronica realized she'd made it even worse.

She took a step closer. "I, ah…just go ahead," she said, sticking her face forward and closing her eyes. Her heart pounded a deep tattoo in her chest.

She expected a quick, businesslike press of his cheek to each of hers, with an air kiss, but instead she felt his large, warm hands on her shoulders as he slowly kissed one hot cheek, then the other. His lips were incongruously soft. Before he stepped back, he said quietly, "I don't mind, either."

She darted a quick, surprised look at him but he had already turned back to sit down, and he put the newspaper back up in front of his face. *Like a paper shield*, she thought.

Jean-Philippe ate a coddled egg, which sat in a little stand painted with a cursive "*J.P.*", dipping buttery fingers of toast into it. He had milky hot cocoa to drink—warm cocoa, really, she knew since she insisted on sipping a spoonful first, just to be sure her little charge didn't burn his mouth—then finished with a miniature chocolate croissant. For her part, Veronica was delighted to have French bread with butter and fresh preserves and a *café au lait* of her own from a mug the size of a medium bowl. The taste made her recall happy memories of grabbing a quick bite before setting out to explore the city of Paris with her friends.

Jean-Philippe kept up a continuous stream of chatter, about animals and plans and songs he liked to sing, until she finally had to laughingly interrupt him to get a word in edgewise.

"All right, if you're finished eating, which I think you must be, let's get our outdoor things on and we'll head out for a walk on the beach," she interjected, and he happily switched gears, hopping down promptly from his chair.

When Alain spoke, she realized that, although he'd appeared to be totally engrossed in what he was doing, switching back and forth from the newspaper to his tablet and cell phone, he must have been listening, too. "The beach on our property? Did Hormet show you the path?"

Veronica nodded. "He said it was an easy climb."

Alain inclined his head in return, the gesture causing a dark lock of hair to fall onto his forehead, making him look suddenly much younger. "It is, and the beach is nice…but mind the tide. It comes in very fast and parts of the beach disappear entirely."

Already standing from her chair, Veronica smiled. "Thank you. I'll keep an eye out."

Jean-Philippe paused on his way to the door and turned back to his father. "Are you coming too, Papa? *Please* say you will!"

Alain opened his mouth, and Veronica could tell he was going to say no, but when he looked at both of them, something changed in his expression, and it went softer somehow. "Papa has to work this morning, *mon grand*, but perhaps I can come meet you with a picnic lunch. How does that sound?"

He spoke to Jean-Philippe, but he looked at Veronica. He wasn't asking permission — she knew intuitively that he wasn't the kind of man who generally asked permission for anything, so used was he to getting his own way and being the master of his own domain — but he was phrasing it as a question out of courtesy and deference to her. She appreciated it.

"Of course," she answered, and Jean-Philippe cheered with excitement.

He practically danced out of the room, and she rushed to follow, only half-turning back to smile at Alain. "See you later. I hope you have a good morning!"

She thought she could feel his warm gaze on her back but knew she was likely just imagining it.

After the pair had left, the breakfast room felt empty. Indeed, the whole house felt emptier. As Alain walked to the wing where he had set up a full home office, complete with a board room and small meeting rooms, fully connected remotely to his company's headquarters and all of the branches, he mused that it was amazing how much life and joy his young son and au pair seemed to exude. He knew that Jean-Philippe could be overwhelming at times, but he got the strong sense that Veronica found him delightful and would know how to take his antics down a notch when needed. She was like a breath of fresh air.

He couldn't help the smile that touched his lips again as he recalled how flamingly red her cheeks had gotten at the idea that he would be kissing her there, and how warm they'd felt beneath his lips. If she'd known how the rest of his body had reacted to the idea, she would have been even more mortified. *Mon Dieu*, his trousers had grown so tight with his sudden and totally inappropriate arousal that he'd had to adjust himself, like he was a student back at *lycée*, high school. He hadn't meant to really press his lips to her cheeks, but when she'd closed her eyes, he hadn't been able to resist. He'd wanted to know if they felt as soft as they'd looked, and in fact, they'd been even softer. It was a long time since he'd found such pleasure in anything so utterly innocent, apart from time he spent with his son.

He was still smiling as he pressed the button in his office that would connect him to his brother via videoconference. Marius sat on one of the white leather couches in his office in their company headquarters in Paris. He wore a charcoal-gray suit and sipped an espresso from a small white cup, and his smile of greeting widened into a grin at Alain's expression.

"*Oh la*, someone is having a good day, I see. What did you have for breakfast, and can I have some too?" His dark eyes, nearly the same color as Alain's own deep-brown eyes, sparkled. It was Marius' secret weapon, in fact, to appear totally at ease and carefree, when in reality, he was incredibly intelligent, and his laughing eyes missed nothing. His brother did genuinely love a good story or joke, though. The number of people Alain trusted to temporarily take over management of his vast company was tiny. In fact, he didn't think he would have trusted anyone besides his brother and their cousin, Magali, particularly not after Sébastien's betrayal. He considered himself lucky, in fact, to have anyone he trusted as much as he did his family.

"Nothing unusual," Alain said, trying to steer Marius away.

"It must have been your companions, then. Didn't you tell me you might hire a new au pair yesterday? Is she stunning? Like maybe she should be on the cover of a magazine and you have no idea how she ended up doing childcare?" There was a hopeful note in Marius' voice, but the image he painted was so opposite to Veronica that Alain answered instinctively.

"No…well, yes." Alain cleared his throat uncomfortably. "I hired the new au pair. But she's…not at all glamorous. Still, she's charming and sweet and…rather delightful." Alain hated the telltale unconscious softening of his voice on the last words.

Marius' smile faded and instead his look grew considering. "That's…unexpected. I want to hear more."

Alain wasn't about to reveal anything else. He couldn't believe he'd admitted as much as he already had. Now, instead of just acting like a callow youth, he sounded like one too…some lovesick schoolboy, which he was so far from that it was laughable. He reminded himself that he'd learned long ago not to trust, because almost everyone eventually betrayed him. He cleared his throat, and when he spoke, his voice was harsher than he'd intended.

"No. We're behind as it is. Let's just get down to business."

Other than raising one eyebrow, Marius looked unfazed and, since he'd known Alain his entire life, he probably *was* as calm as he looked. Whereas most people Alain worked with were either a little afraid or in awe of him, which was the way he generally preferred it, his brother knew him well enough to recognize what was part of the act and what was really Alain. Still, Marius dutifully set down his afternoon coffee and picked up the sheaf of papers on the desk in front of him.

"Let's dive right in, then, shall we?" Marius said, picking up with the first item that required Alain's personal review and approval. Something in the tilt of his chin, though, warned Alain that he hadn't forgotten his older brother's impulsive comments about Veronica. *Great.* Putting it out of his mind, Alain turned his attention to the latest potential setback to a key acquisition of a competitor company, currently valued at several hundred-million euros.

Chapter Six

The walk down to the private beach was as easy as Monsieur Hormet and Alain had said, even with the bulging bag of beach toys and other playthings that Jean-Philippe had insisted they just *had to* bring, along with towels, water and plenty of sunblock. In spite of the cool temperature — or maybe even because of it — Veronica knew she'd have to be extra careful to reapply sunblock frequently to avoid them both getting boiled like Maine lobsters. Jean-Philippe had obviously not inherited his father's darker, Mediterranean complexion, but instead had very fair skin, not unlike her own. After she'd coated them both with sunscreen and affixed a wide-brimmed hat onto a squirming bundle of Jean-Philippe, she let him run loose. He scampered up and down the beach, calling her over to look at snails and crabs, darting minnows that came close to his feet and countless seagulls, which he never seemed to grow tired of chasing.

She'd laid their large plaid blanket, provided by the almost-prescient Hormet, under a shady outcropping, and they sat there for a while, too, as she taught Jean-Philippe some songs, which he was delighted by, and they built a large sandcastle together. When she'd rinsed her hands in the freezing ocean water and wiped them off on her pants, then dug her cell phone out of her pocket, she was shocked to see that it was already a little after noon.

Shielding her eyes with her hand and squinting against the midday sun, she didn't see any sign of Alain. She wasn't too concerned, though, since she'd guessed that they might have a somewhat-later lunch, given how French the rest of the household customs seemed to be, so she herded her little charge toward the tide pools nearby.

The pools were as full of animals as she'd hoped, with hermit crabs, sea anemones, red sea stars and even a spiky purple sea urchin. As Jean-Philippe squatted, delighted to look at everything and assuring her he knew not to touch anything, she kept her watchful gaze on his little form and let half her mind drift back to the morning, to Alain's kissing her on the cheeks. She knew she shouldn't make a big deal out of it, but…she'd been greeted with kisses before many times when she'd studied in France. He hadn't needed to hold her shoulders or let his lips touch her cheeks. Her whole body had reacted at the simple touch, making her breathless and hot. She'd wanted to fan herself afterward. It had affected her that much. What had he meant by it? And why had she reacted so strongly? Her new employer was a strange mixture of charming and worldly, gruff and prickly. He was stunningly gentle with his son, but he'd also been oddly distant, especially when he'd abruptly left before dinner the night before.

She was startled out of her thoughts when Jean-Philippe gave a joyful cry, springing to his feet and pointing behind her. She spun around to see Alain's tall form, making his slow, deliberate way across the beach with his walk that favored one leg. He was dressed casually — or at least, probably casually for him — in light-colored slacks and a collared shirt with a button-down cable-knit sweater loosely fastened over it. The wind had mussed his thick hair, so that he looked somehow younger, and the effect was devastating. She could have sworn her heart actually squeezed in her chest at how handsome he looked. Then her heart sped for a different reason. To her dismay, she saw that the tide had come in considerably in the brief time she and Jean-Philippe had been at the tide pools, and they were now standing on a sort of island surrounded by shallow water. Alain had warned her. Her face flushed crimson with embarrassment, and she bit her lip, worried that he was going to think she was incredibly careless, especially on her first full day.

"*Papa!*" Jean-Philippe called as Alain got within shouting distance, waving his arm so hard she thought he might topple over with the force.

"Ahoy, my son!" Alain called back, his face splitting into a large smile that made his eyes crinkle at the corners.

"And Veronica, too! We're looking at tidepool creatures. There's so many to see, Papa! I never realized!"

"Ahoy to Veronica as well, of course," Alain replied, stopping near where the waves were now lapping farther and farther up the beach. "I'm glad you are seeing and learning so much."

Veronica looked down to where the water nearly touched his canvas shoes. Good Lord, this was mortifying.

"I'm so sorry. I was watching the tide, but...you weren't kidding when you said it came in fast. It's only been about five minutes since I last checked." She felt terrible, and her apology was heartfelt.

Alain's smile was lopsided, and her heart flip-flopped. "It's happened to all of us. My younger brother and I were once stuck for a number of hours right over there, on top of that rock." He gestured toward a large, smooth boulder not too far from where they stood. "Our parents just thought we were having a great time and didn't come to look for us until sunset. We'd thought we were watching too."

Relief flooded her that he didn't seem furious.

"We do need to get you down, though," Alain continued, eyeing the rising water. She and Jean-Philippe were wearing their shoes, to protect their feet from the hard rocks, but she didn't mind getting hers wet.

"Oh, no problem, I'll just climb down into the water and I can carry Jean-Philippe across," she called. "Jean-Philippe, can you come here?" She held out her hand, and the little boy obediently took it and came closer to her, careful to avoid the tidepools, although taking a last, lingering look at the animals.

Alain pursed his lips and shook his head in a gesture she recognized as being a distinctly French form of mild disagreement. "No need. Just hand him to me, then I'll come back and grab you." He slipped his shoes off as he spoke, leaving them on a rock next to him so they wouldn't get wet, then he waded through the shallow water which was getting deeper by the minute.

"I, ah, well, sure," she said, utterly surprised by the unexpected picture he made, the perfectly polished businessman going right into the water. "But there's no need to carry me. I'll just slide down on my own."

"Go ahead and jump, *petit*. I'll catch you," Alain urged his son, who grinned and leapt right into his father's arms. Veronica thought she saw him wince slightly when he took the full brunt of Jean-Philippe's weight, but the expression was gone almost before she saw it, and there was no limp when he made his careful way back to the dry part of the beach, so she thought he must be all right. Still, she wasn't going to let him try to carry her heavier weight, so she began to scrabble down the rocks as quickly as possible. Just when she thought she was nearly down, though, her foot slipped and wedged itself right into a little crevice, and she couldn't seem to get it out.

When Alain turned back after setting Jean-Philippe down a good distance up onto the sand, beyond where the high tide mark was, he didn't say anything, but he quirked one dark eyebrow up questioningly.

"I, ah, tried to get down, but now my foot is stuck," she said lamely.

"The rocks are slippery," he acknowledged, but there was a distinct amusement behind his dry tone.

As he got closer, wading into water that was now splashing up to his thighs, Veronica felt her heartbeat quicken. Every part of her was aware of him, so strong and masculine. Solid. When he reached her side, he pushed back his sleeves, revealing large forearms, corded with muscles and dusted with small dark hairs that nearly sparkled in the sun. He reached down and loosened the rocks that trapped her foot, but when he straightened, she noticed that there were angry red scars all along the underside of his arm. She couldn't quite stop her quick intake of air, and his dark gaze shot to hers, suddenly blank and totally guarded. She didn't say anything and the moment passed, but Alain still looked more distant than he had. Closed.

"Put your arms around my neck," he said gruffly.

"It's all right. I can walk now, I think," she answered, but he shook his head.

"Not until I look at that ankle. Now come on. It's getting deeper every second." He sounded cold now, much more like the austere man she'd met the day before. She wanted to disagree, but he had a point. She put her arms around his neck, and he pulled her to him.

He was warm, almost like a toasty oven in contrast to the icy ocean water, and every part of him felt firm and strong. She'd never thought to be this close to him, and here she was, not only near him but cradled in his arms. Her breath quickened and her body tingled everywhere they touched. Her nipples beaded to hard points of awareness, making her blush, and she hoped he couldn't feel them through their sweaters. She saw that his dark beard stubble was just starting to show on his chin, and when she inhaled, she was surrounded by his scent, a mix of spicy and masculine. She could have happily stayed there forever, but as soon as they neared the dry beach, she leapt down, anxious not to take advantage any more than she had.

He grunted with what sounded like pain, and she spun back to look at him in concern.

"I'm so sorry! Did carrying me hurt you?"

His expression was dark for a moment then closed off again. "I'm perfectly well, thank you. Your ankle looks like it's taking your weight nicely, now, too, so no concerns there. Now that we've had our adventure for the day, let's go check out the picnic that I brought. Jean-Philippe. Eveline packed several of your favorites."

The little boy whooped with happiness, oblivious to the undercurrents between his father and Veronica — or maybe not as oblivious as it seemed when he spoke again.

"Veronica, you just have to be careful of Papa's side and especially his leg, because he was burned in the accident. But we don't talk about it." He delivered that contradictory statement in a helpful tone with a large smile and ran off down the beach, toward their blanket where a large basket had now joined her bag.

Veronica was brimming with questions about the accident. What had happened? Why? Was it connected to Jean-Philippe's mother's death? She darted a glance at Alain's face, and his expression was remote. She sighed inwardly, swallowing her questions and respecting his unspoken request not to mention it further. She of all people understood that there were some areas of memory, of the past, that were just too painful to explore.

When he winced as he began to reach down for his shoes, she jumped to grab them and handed them to him. She commented simply, "Thank you again for helping me, and thank you for bringing a picnic. I know Jean-Philippe will love it. He was talking all morning about how he couldn't wait to see you."

With that, along with a tentative smile, she gave him the space and time to make his way to the blanket, and she hurried after Jean-Philippe's small form to try to set up the picnic before he covered all the food with sand from his excited little fingers.

Alain's leg hurt like the devil as he made his way across the beach, trailing Jean-Philippe and Veronica, and he knew he'd pay heavily later once he'd sat down and stopped moving. In fact, he would have to be careful to keep shifting his leg as they ate their picnic. *Dieu merci*, he'd brought folding chairs along with the basket. It had made the walk more awkward, but at least he wouldn't be stuck, too stiff to stand up off the sand. He hated showing any weakness to anyone, but in front of his son's young au pair, it rankled especially. The pain and stiffness, coupled with the hard, shiny skin that stretched too tight over his scars, were a constant, daily reminder of how much Joëlle had hated him in the end, which was particularly painful since he'd once loved her with what he'd thought was all his heart.

As he watched Veronica catch up to Jean-Philippe, sinking to her knees with a grace and ease he envied and deftly taking over the unpacking of all the picnic items in such a way that made his son still feel happy and included, he felt a lightness in the area of his heart that he seldom felt around anyone except his son. He didn't understand why he felt such a curious mix of emotions around her and what about her prompted him to speak of things — personal things — that he never usually trusted anyone enough to mention. He'd told her about his father's family last night, then today, he'd told her about how he and Marius had once been stranded. He couldn't fathom the reason. Also, he should have been angry — or at least annoyed — with her for being so careless about the tide. But when he'd seen her earnest, apologetic face, so guileless, he'd felt the strangest urge to comfort instead of scold her.

It wasn't as if she were incredibly glamorous or irresistible — quite the opposite, in fact. Oh, he knew she thought she probably looked suitable — neat and practical — and her pants and sweater were definitely sturdy enough to withstand a day with Jean-Philippe, but they did nothing in particular to flatter her generous curves. He was still trying to forget how good those curves had felt briefly pressed against him — totally inappropriate for an employer to be thinking about his employee. At the sensation of the soft mounds of her breasts against his chest, he had hardened again almost painfully for the second time that day, the reaction as surprising and unwelcome as it had been that morning. He hadn't felt a stirring of sexual attraction for anyone since the accident, but now, to feel it for his own young female employee was nothing less than shocking. For a second, he'd thought he might have felt her tremble as her nipples had brushed his chest, but he must have imagined it.

With her hair blowing everywhere in the wind and her cheeks and eyes bright with excitement, she did have a wholesome charm, though, nothing like the usual polished society ladies he saw at countless parties and events throughout Europe, tall and willowy with impeccable make-up, artfully coiffed and clad in the very height of fashionable gowns and high heels. That must be it, he reasoned. Veronica was totally different from the women he had become used to spending time with. His cousin, Magali, was probably his closest female friend, and even she wore designer suits to work and designer yacht-wear when she was being 'casual'. His late wife…well, Joëlle, had refused to buy almost anything off the rack, preferring only haute couture pieces, which she'd ordered directly from designers at fashion shows. He ought to know. He'd paid all the bills. Even her lingerie had been custom ordered. The now-familiar rage welled inside of him when he recalled that she'd always told him she wanted to make him proud of her, proud to be her husband, but in reality, she'd been looking good for everyone else instead. For *Sébastien*.

He took a deep breath, forcing himself to calm and return to the present. His wife and friend were gone, but Jean-Philippe and Veronica were here, and his son was excited to spend time with him. He needed to remember that. He forced a smile he wasn't sure he felt, but it turned more genuine as Jean-Philippe popped up and ran to him, hugging him tightly.

"Thank you, Papa! I'm so e'cited to eat my favorite olives! And orange fizzy soda... Yum, yum, *yum*!"

He chuckled. "But not together, right?"

Jean-Philippe cocked his head, considering. "Maaaaybe, but I think I want the baguette and cheese with the olives, then the soda. Not that gross wine you brought, though. *Ew*." He eyed the small-batch artisanal *vendanges tardives* white wine that Alain had thrown in to accompany the little tartlets for dessert with open disgust. Alain had to smother a laugh.

"That sounds great, *mon chou*. And the wine is for Veronica and me. That is, if she'd like some?" He noted with a satisfaction that made him feel warmer than he had any right to feel that she'd set out the two folding chairs he'd brought, and she'd already made a plate for each of them.

She looked at the wine and a little crinkle appeared in her forehead. "I don't know a lot about wine, but that one looks nice, so you might not want to waste it on me. My best friend Katrin and I usually just get the screw-top Australian wine from the grocery store when we're having a girls' night."

Alain hid his amusement at the comparison between the small bottle of incomparable and exquisite white wine, made from the last grapes of the season when they were at their sweetest, and 'screw-top Australian wine'. Good manners and a real desire — strange as it was — to make her feel more comfortable and to make up for his earlier gruffness prompted him to say, "Please...I insist. I just hope you enjoy it."

He grabbed the bottle and glasses before he eased himself slowly into the folding chair, his leg already protesting. *Oui*, it was going to be a painful night. Veronica dug around in the basket and her face was apologetic when she finished, empty-handed. She should never play poker, he thought. She would lose miserably.

"Sorry, but the corkscrew must have been left out."

He shook his head. "Ah, *non*. I always carry this with me," he said, producing a deluxe Swiss army knife from his pocket and flipping out first a tiny knife, to cut away the thin metal covering over the cork, then flipping out the corkscrew to remove the cork itself. She watched him — actually, she and Jean-Philippe both did — so he felt like he was putting on a fascinating show instead of performing a simple act. It was oddly endearing. When he pulled the cork out with a pop, Jean-Philippe clapped and Veronica looked like she wanted to.

"Bravo, Papa. You're very fast with that tool!" Jean-Philippe enthused.

Alain couldn't help another chuckle that escaped.

Veronica, sitting back on her heels with one hand still absently placed on the picnic basket, tilted her head to one side. "I've always wondered if there was really that much call in the Swiss army for opening wine bottles. Definitely must be a different sort of army from the American one."

Alain could see why she got along so well with his inquisitive little son. Her mind seemed to wander along the same lines. "Well, the corkscrew has numerous uses, including removing bullets, but historically wine was something most European armies—and everyone else who could—drank. Wine or ale was safer than water. They still serve breakfast beers in Belgium. They have a very low alcohol content. Did your travels not take you to Switzerland?"

It was as if a cloud passed over her face, and she was silent so long that he thought she might not answer, but finally she did. "I had a lot of plans to travel in the summer, but then...I suddenly had to come home."

"I see," he said, and although he didn't know what she referred to, he did see the sorrow plainly written on her face. Whatever reason she'd had to go home for hadn't been a good one. It caused her pain even now. That was something he could recognize.

It was odd that he cared so much, but for whatever reason, he didn't want to see the sadness in her eyes. It bothered him on a deeper level than he ever would have expected, so he hastened to change the subject.

"Is that plate for me?" he asked gently, gesturing toward one of the larger plates that she'd set on the blanket. It obviously was—Jean-Philippe had his and was already munching away—but she smiled gratefully and nodded, as if it hadn't been a totally superfluous question.

"Yes, I gave you a bit of everything. It all looks delicious."

He stretched out his hand to take the plate, and his fingers just brushed hers as she handed it to him. Their skin, where it touched, set off a riot of sensations in him. He pulled back as if he'd been burned, and an olive rolled off the plate onto the sand. She followed it with her eyes but didn't say anything.

They ate their meal mostly in companionable silence, although Jean-Philippe interjected several comments. Alain didn't understand why he felt so drawn to the little au pair, but then also felt so intensely uncomfortable when he was with her. Her clear gaze, so artless, without hidden agenda, seemed to see more of him than he wanted her to, more than he wanted anyone to. As soon as he possibly could, he stood, brushing crumbs off his lap and finishing the last of his wine.

Jean-Philippe came next to Alain, taking his father's hand into his chubby, sticky fingers. "Yay!" the little boy said. "Now we can go back to the tidepools together!"

Alain hated to disappoint his son, but he needed to get away from them. Perhaps he was as hard and heartless as he'd been called often enough, but he couldn't stand it. He didn't feel worthy of the clear-eyed adulation that Jean-Philippe always showed him.

"I'm sorry, *mon fils*, but I have afternoon videoconferences, mostly with contacts on the American West Coast. I may not see you at dinner." He spoke to Jean-Philippe but also vaguely in Veronica's direction. He knew she'd understand not to wait for him.

"Don't clean up," he ordered, his tone much more strident than he'd intended. He didn't like to see her gathering everything up, which she would struggle to carry up alone, but his leg was burning, and he knew he'd be pushing it to walk up himself. He'd been overconfident, leaving his cane behind. A little too proud for his own good, wanting to carry the basket himself.

She froze and put her hands behind herself unconsciously.

"There's no need," he continued, trying for a softer tone. "I'll ask Eveline and Yvette to come down. You go ahead and enjoy yourselves. Eveline would never forgive me if I let you take care of this. She has very old-fashioned ideas."

Veronica nodded, but her eyes were a little wary. Jean-Philippe was wearing his stoic face again, and Alain's heart turned over in his chest, but he didn't stay. He couldn't.

"*À tout à l'heure*," he finished. *See you soon.* But he didn't know if he would. Still, tomorrow was soon enough, wasn't it? He turned without waiting for a response and limped back up the path.

* * * *

That night at bedtime, Jean-Philippe was full of questions.

"Didn't we have a wonderful day, Veronica? Can we go to the beach tomorrow? And the next day? And the next day?"

Veronica laughed as she wiped toothpaste off his face.

"I don't know about tomorrow, but we can go again soon. It was definitely wonderful," she answered, and it had been. She had genuinely enjoyed almost every moment.

Jean-Philippe looked at her reflection in the mirror, catching her eyes with his in their images. "Do you think Papa will come again tomorrow?"

She inwardly sighed, unsure how to answer. Alain was as contradictory as ever. He'd been so carefree and kind at breakfast, then again when he'd brought the picnic down to them on the beach, but when he'd left, he'd felt cold and remote. For her own part, she wasn't crazy about trying to figure out which Alain to expect—it was uncomfortable—but she hated it for Jean-Philippe. The little boy obviously adored his father, and Alain just as obviously adored his child, so she wasn't sure why he was cutting himself off. He hadn't even eaten dinner with them, had just come in briefly to excuse himself and say goodnight to Jean-Philippe, then she'd heard him speaking English with someone on a conference call when they'd walked by.

"I'm not sure if your papa will have time to come, *chéri*, but I'm sure he'll come if he's able to," she said carefully, and Jean-Philippe seemed satisfied with that answer.

As she tucked him in, he squirmed until he was comfortable.

"Can I hear more of the story about the beast and Ludo?" he asked, and Veronica beamed, surprised and delighted that he remembered so much of what she'd told him the night before. She sat down in the chair next to his bed.

"Of course! Where were we?"

He turned his head on his pillow, making his blond curls fan out behind his head, and looked at her seriously. "Ludo was stuck in a gully, and the beast was going to rescue him."

"Ah, of course! Thank you for reminding me. All right... Ludo stopped crying when he saw the beast looking down at him, but not because he was relieved. No, Ludo was so afraid of how scary the beast looked that he grew silent with terror. But that was actually a good thing because he discovered something no one else knew — "

"What was it?" Jean-Philippe prompted excitedly.

"That the beast could talk," Veronica finished, poking him teasingly on the nose with one finger. "He had always been able to talk, but little Ludo was the first one to listen. The beast asked" — Veronica made her voice growly and low for the next part — "'why are you crying, little child?'"

"Do Ludo's voice, too!" Jean-Philippe ordered, and Veronica complied with a higher voice for the fictional Ludo.

"'I was picking berries, but I went farther than I'm allowed — everyone knows we're supposed to stay away from your castle — but I fell and got stuck, and now I'm cold and hungry and you're going to eat me!'"

Jean-Philippe's eyes went wide, and Veronica shook her head.

"Don't worry," she said, then switched back to the beast's voice. "'I'm not going to eat you, little boy. I'm not in the habit of eating children. It's getting dark, and it's too dangerous for you to be out, so I will help you in any case. But I do hope you might consider doing me a favor in return.'

"Now, Ludo was a fair-minded little boy, and he was also very relieved to not be being eaten, so of course he agreed, and the beast picked him up like he was a feather and took the little boy back to his castle."

"What was the favor?" Jean-Philippe murmured sleepily, but Veronica held up a staying finger.

"You'll find out tomorrow night," she promised, and he drifted off, his breathing becoming slow and even before she slipped silently out of his room and back to her own.

Later, with her hair washed and lying in bed, she pulled out her phone. It felt intrusive, but she really wanted to know what 'accident' had happened to Alain and Jean-Philippe, although she got the sense that it hadn't been accidental. It would help her steer clear of things she shouldn't bring up if she knew what they were. She hoped maybe she could look up whoever 'the beast' was, too, but she was thwarted by bad reception again as the Internet browser on her phone just gave her the 'loading' message and never loaded. She sighed and lay back, going over everything that had happened.

There had been an accident, and Alain had been injured. His wife, Jean-Philippe's mother, had been in an accident too, but with someone named Sébastien, and she'd died. She wondered if Alain had loved her very much, to have seemingly closed down when Jean-Philippe mentioned her. Actually, though…when she thought about it, Alain had seemed all right with Jean-Philippe mentioning his mother's death. But he'd gotten that scary, dark expression when Sébastien, whoever he was, had been mentioned. There was obviously more to this than it seemed. Did Veronica possibly remind him of his late wife? Was that part of the problem? She didn't know how much she could have in common with a woman who had probably been incredibly glamorous, to capture the eye and heart of someone like Alain. His wife must have been extremely wealthy, if not before she'd married Alain then certainly after.

Veronica rolled from one side to the other, trying to get better reception on her phone and finally giving up. She wasn't going to go outside in her nightgown, for heaven's sake. Not tonight anyway. Maybe tomorrow she'd resort to more extreme measures. Actually, she could just text Katrin, since texts would eventually go through…but somehow that felt wrong, like she didn't want to pry into things he didn't want her to know.

Without conscious thought, instead of pressing Katrin's name, she pressed another name. Gabe. She didn't know exactly where he was or when he would get the message, but still she typed.

Miss u, stinkface. Went to the beach and thought of u and Troy today.

Before she could talk herself out of it, she hit send.

It took her a long time to fall asleep, but when she did, she dreamed of happy times, running along the beach in the South of France with the odd group of Jean-Philippe, Alain, Gabe and Troy. When she woke up, realizing too slowly that it wasn't real, grief speared through her like it sometimes still did, even after all this time, and she curled into a ball, letting the tears flow. She resolved that they would stay away from the beach for a while.

Chapter Seven

The next day dawned cool and rainy, with billowing black clouds hanging ominously over the ocean. The weather didn't dim Jean-Philippe's spirits at all, though, as he woke Veronica up as he had the morning before. At least this time she was prepared and didn't scream.

At breakfast, Alain was polite but quiet. Distant. He greeted his son warmly, and also kissed her on the cheeks, just as he had done the day before, making her heart thump and her cheeks heat. After that, however, it was as if he had put up an invisible wall…or shield. Surrounded by his tablet, phone and the newspaper again, he might as well have set up a little satellite office at the table.

"Are we going to the beach again?" Jean-Philippe asked before stuffing two toast fingers into his mouth and taking a swig of chocolate milk.

"Sorry, buddy. I think the weather isn't nice enough, but we can still go outside. I saw a little pond we can walk to. Do you maybe want to go look for frogs? The animals love the rain, you know."

The little boy's face, which had drooped a bit, brightened right back up.

"Oh, yes! Can we? Won't we get wet? Can I splash in puddles?"

Veronica had to laugh. He was just so refreshing and enthusiastic about almost everything. "We'll wear raincoats and boots and bring umbrellas, although frankly, I usually find those more of a bother than anything since they get turned inside out if it's windy and you still get wet. You can totally splash in a few puddles, as long as they're not crazy deep."

Jean-Philippe cheered, and Alain raised one dark eyebrow. Even though he appeared absorbed in his work, she thought he might still be listening.

"Then maybe this afternoon we can spend some time in the Music Room…or at least, I think that's what Monsieur Hormet called it on my tour of the house."

Jean-Philippe wrinkled his forehead. "What are we going to do there?"

"Well, I know you liked some of the songs we sang yesterday, so I thought you might like to hear them on a piano—and maybe some more too. Have you ever played the piano?" Veronica watched his face, trying to gauge his interest. Jean-Philippe's eyes sparkled.

"That sounds *fantastique*! I like to sing. My papa plays the violin with me. Or he used to, until *Maman* told him she hated it. Do you really think my voice is, um, *grinçante et dénué de talent*? That means un-pleasing, right? Lacking talent?"

Veronica froze, unsure how best to respond, especially since the little boy's translations were probably a little softer than the real words, but Jean-

Philippe continued without waiting for an answer, speaking the next thought that had obviously occurred to him. "Papa, will you come play with us, too? Please don't say no."

As Veronica and Jean-Philippe both turned to look at him, Alain's face was set in stone. In fact, Veronica thought his whole body might be frozen, but with what, it wasn't clear. Behind his dark eyes, though, she detected shock and what might have been well-concealed anger. He stood abruptly, making his chair squeak along the marble floor behind him, and Veronica's heart fell. It seemed like she was going to get gruff Alain again, and Jean-Philippe was going to continue to be disappointed. But he surprised her by answering.

"You have a beautiful voice, *mon fils*. I'll rearrange some meetings so I can join you for a while...maybe around one-thirty or so?" The last was vaguely directed at Veronica, clearly not really a question but a polite demand.

"Perfect," she answered unnecessarily, smiling brightly. Alain's curt nod was her response, but as he passed by her, she saw something in his expression that looked oddly like regret. Deep, vast regret. Then he was gone.

Jean-Philippe smiled broadly at her, finishing his food with gusto. "Yesterday was the best day ever, and today is going to be the best day ever, too!" he enthused.

Veronica didn't correct that impossible statement. "You know, I think you may be right," she laughed, making him giggle when she ruffled his soft hair.

* * * *

Upstairs in Alain's office, Marius' smiling face popped up on the large flatscreen monitor as he connected their daily check-in videoconference, but his brother's smile faded quickly at his expression.

"Uh-oh, I'd say good morning, but obviously, it's not so good for you," Marius quipped, sipping a mineral water this time. "Did I miss something bad as the US markets opened? I just got out of a long meeting. I don't know how you stand some of these things."

Alain grunted. "Give me a minute. I just…" He sighed, running his hand through his hair. "If I ask you something, will you answer honestly?"

Marius sat back on the couch behind him, crossing one leg on top of the other, and his expression grew even more concerned. "Of course."

His brother was one of the few people Alain had told about how Joëlle had really died. He'd never come out and said everything, but he thought Marius had guessed some — or maybe even most of it. Certainly not all of it, though. But still, even knowing all that he did, Alain had been shocked to hear Jean-Philippe repeat the harsh words at the breakfast table, which had obviously been spoken to the little boy by his mother. He shouldn't have been.

"Do you think Joëlle loved Jean-Philippe?" Alain asked the question that he thought he might be afraid to know the real answer to.

Marius looked grave, and he took a moment to think, tapping his lower lip with his index finger. "I think she cared for him as much as she cared for anyone who wasn't herself. So yes, in her own way, I imagine that she did."

It was better than he'd expected, but still not enough. He had owed more to the little boy who was probably currently putting on rain boots and practically hopping with excitement at the prospect of splashing in puddles.

"Why didn't I see who she was? *What* she was? I have sniffed out every corporate spy, figured out what the breaking point price for every business owner is in order to finalize a merger or acquisition. *Zut*, I even exposed Magali's last boyfriend for the fortune-hunter he was, and he seemed so genuine." Alain hated this feeling. Just when he thought he knew all of the worst, he heard something new about Joëlle to break his heart all over again. How could she have told Jean-Philippe that she thought his voice was annoying? What could be more joyful than a child who loved to sing with his father?

Even though Marius was only on a screen, across the Atlantic, Alain felt his brother's sympathy, and Marius didn't yet know the full story.

"Even the keenest of us are sometimes blinded by love, it seems. I don't think any of us saw her for the cold operator she turned out to be, if it helps," his brother answered.

Alain thought back to all the holidays, parties, even just all of the damn dinners at home he'd shared with his late wife. He'd known they'd had some problems, yes. He'd seen it was difficult for her to warm up to their child, but he'd made excuses for her in his mind. She wasn't the maternal type, after all. She'd always been more about fun and glamour than anything else, and he'd once loved that about her. She'd been focused on her position in society, he'd told himself, to advance their whole family. But how had he missed how truly unkind she'd been to her own child?

He shook his head, forcing his thoughts back to the present. "*Bon*, well, dwelling on it won't change it. Let's talk about the latest on Project Cygne."

Marius was silent for a moment. "Let me know if you'd like for me to come visit, *frangin*," he offered, using a French nickname for brother. "Magali can helm the ship for a few days, and it's always a good time to hang out with you and my brilliant little nephew. I can check out your sweet new nanny, too."

Alain was touched by his brother's words, and he actually might love a visit. But oddly, the idea of shy and genuine Veronica, so seemingly unaffected, meeting his elegant, handsome brother, who had no limp and an easy way with women he'd had since birth, made something dark rear its head in Alain's chest. It felt almost like possessiveness, which he had absolutely no right to.

"I'll keep that in my back pocket for when I need it," he finally answered, and they got down to the agenda items Marius had emailed earlier.

* * * *

The morning's excursion and a delicious warm lunch passed quickly. Veronica had learned early — first as a big sister, then when she'd been a babysitter and nanny in high school and college — that it was best to take young kids outdoors every day, if at all possible, and to always keep them engaged in some way. She truly enjoyed the way preschoolers thought, and already her conversations with Jean-Philippe had reminded her of how imaginative and curious they were. She'd missed that, working as she had been in the corporate world. She hadn't realized just how much she'd missed it. Jean-Philippe seemed particularly bright, and wow, did he have a memory like a steel trap. She'd stubbed her toe on a rock, walking back from the pond, and almost uttered something inappropriate.

Without missing a beat, Jean-Philippe had looked up at her with wide eyes. "Were you going to say something bad? Nanny Marie said that you should always behave as if God were listening to every word. Although once, when she tripped and fell on the stone floor, she said something that I don't think God would approve of. It was definitely loud enough for Him to hear. But on the other hand, if He invented all the words, then He must know that people need to say them sometimes, right?"

Veronica had stared, speechless, and she couldn't fault his logic. Luckily, as it had earlier in the day, his brain had moved on before she had needed to say anything, but she had no doubt that he had stored away the incident and would never forget it.

Now, as they headed to the Music Room, she thought again of Jean-Philippe's comments that morning and Alain's reaction. It was shocking that his mother had apparently used those exact words, directly to or in the hearing of her three- or four-year-old child. Veronica hated to think ill of the dead, and she was willing to give Jean-Phillipe's mother the benefit of the doubt in many things but…what she'd said had been incredibly harsh. Alain, though, had reacted as though he were both surprised and resigned. Something more complicated than just a normal grieving process was going on, but she just wasn't sure what it was. Still, she was glad Alain had indicated he would join them, but she was also worried that he wouldn't come. Or, if he did, that she would continue to have the same strange reaction to him.

Oh, she'd known handsome men before. She'd dated in college, and sporadically afterward, but had never really clicked with anyone. Every young man — and most of the older ones, too — just seemed almost too frivolous — like they were worried about keeping up with the local professional sports teams and who had the best deals on drinks or how to get ahead in their careers. Normal stuff. They liked to talk about the things that were important to them, which was totally understandable, but she just couldn't muster that much enthusiasm for most of it. With the sorrow in her past, she just felt strongly that she didn't want to waste much of the precious time that she had on this Earth on things that didn't really spark anything in her beyond the superficial or on anyone she felt that way about. Added to the fact that she wasn't that interested, she'd been told a few times that she was 'cute but not beautiful'.

Katrin had assured her that she would someday soon find 'the one' who would see beyond her serious façade, and Veronica tried to believe her closest friend, but it wasn't easy. In fact, she'd been disappointed a few too many times, so she'd stopped looking very hard, at least for a while. But Alain Reynard was a man who she couldn't stop looking at, couldn't seem to stop her body from reacting to. He was mysterious and contradictory and all sorts of things that screamed 'complicated', but that only made her more curious, more drawn to him. Whatever he was — and she suspected there were strong undercurrents under his generally controlled mask and even under the emotions he had allowed to shine through — he wasn't superficial. All that depth was wrapped up in a gorgeous exterior so that her heart pounded almost out of her chest whenever he was close. Whenever he was in the same room, even.

She told herself, not for the first time, that she just needed to stay calm and professional. She would be prepared this time, and thus avoid the worst of her reaction. She sat down at the piano, and Jean-Philippe, heedless of personal space in the way of young children, slid right next to her on the piano bench. She began playing several of her favorite songs, starting with something simple.

Jean-Philippe seemed totally absorbed and genuinely interested, which made it easy for her to keep going. After a few English folk songs, he begged her for one in French, and she agreed readily. Unfortunately, she realized that most of the songs she knew in French were more classical, but she guessed he'd probably enjoy one of them too, since he seemed so interested.

She mentally selected a Debussy song that she knew all the words to, remembering about halfway through the second line that it was actually quite sad. It started off about the evening and dreams, but the undertones were of sorrow and loss. It wasn't exactly the best thing to play for a four-year-old who'd lost his mother. Her fingers slowed on the keys, and his face looked crestfallen. Quickly considering, she thought he probably wouldn't catch the undertones. He might not even know all the vocabulary yet, either. Still, she stopped after the end of the first verse, pretending it was over.

A noise behind them made her spin around, her heart in her throat, to see the tall, distinguished form that was becoming achingly familiar to her. Alain's face wore an expression that she thought must have contributed to his incredible success in business, and which gave away absolutely nothing of his inner thoughts. Still, she flushed guiltily.

"Papa!" Jean-Philippe cried happily. "Veronica is totally awesome, isn't she? We learned lots of English songs. I just begged her to play one in French, too, and she *did*! Isn't she cool?"

At the somewhat slangy phrasing, Alain raised an eyebrow, and she thought she saw amusement now behind his dark eyes.

"Definitely, er, awesome," Alain agreed with his son, then turned to Veronica. "You really do play and sing beautifully. A bit…heavy for the audience though, no?" he commented.

Her fingers were still on the keys, and she pressed several notes inadvertently, echoing the last chord again before she pulled her hands into her lap. She shrugged apologetically. "I'm afraid that I know a lot more songs in English. I never took music when I studied in France, and when I was younger and taking lessons, I was rather…high-brow and serious. Probably a little too serious." *Yikes, where had that come from?* She was telling Alain way more than she normally would. Probably way more than he wanted to know.

He didn't look bored, though. For a second, he looked almost intrigued, as if he might ask another question, but then Jean-Philippe fidgeted and Alain closed his mouth.

"We can fix that, can't we, *mon chou*?" he said, instead of whatever he had been going to say, including his son in his hearty declaration. Jean-Philippe nodded an enthusiastic response.

Veronica started to stand, but Alain's large hand, warm and firm even through her thick sweater, stayed her gently.

"Please, stay right there. It will be easier for you to learn by playing along. I'll take out my violin."

Jean-Philippe clapped, his delight now totally obvious and infectious. Veronica found a grin spreading across her own face as well.

"Of course. That sounds great," she answered. "It's awesome that you play, too."

Alain's answering smile warmed her everywhere, and she didn't think she'd ever seen him look so at ease. "It's one of my favorite things...one of *our* favorite things, in fact." His expression darkened then and hardened. "Or, it was," he continued in a clipped voice.

Veronica held her breath unconsciously, wondering if he was going to reveal more about his late wife, anything to excuse her behavior, but he stopped and shook his head instead.

"And there's no reason that it shouldn't be again, especially now," he finished, offering a tenuous smile to his little son. Jean-Philippe nodded emphatically, his curls bouncing around his face.

"Let's teach Veronica everything! Can we, Papa? She has to know all the songs. Everyone should know French songs, shouldn't they? French songs are the *best!*" He paused, Veronica thought only because he had to draw breath, then kept going. "With hand gestures. The hand gestures are *très important*," he said, slipping into French in his excitement and waving his hands around.

Alain chuckled, and ruffled his son's hair. "So true, my boy. But they will be difficult for Veronica to do if she is using her hands to play the piano. Why don't you stand over there" — he gestured to an open area on the carpeting — "and do all the movements so she can see them, for later?"

Jean-Philippe looked abashed for about a millisecond, then hopped down, standing exactly where Alain had pointed. "Yes, Veronica, you can watch me. Right here. I'll be *right here*. The hand gestures are super important, for later." He echoed his father's words nearly exactly, and Veronica hid another smile.

When she looked up, Alain's amused gaze caught and held hers from across the room, where he'd gone to retrieve his violin. Her breath hitched and her pulse fluttered wildly. Every time she'd seen him, she'd thought he was attractive. Incredibly so. Now, in this moment of lighthearted harmony, enjoying the exuberance of his little boy, he was also accessible in a way he'd never seemed to be before. Like she could really be his friend…or something else.

Then, as before, his face grew closed again, but she had seen the distinctive flash of guilt. *Why guilt?* She wondered. *About what?*

They played several fast songs, most of which had very definite hand gestures for Jean-Philippe. He grew flushed with joy, giggling so hard he had trouble singing, but undeterred for all of that. His favorite seemed to be *Sur le Pont d'Avignon*, On the Bridge of Avignon, since then he could call out things for the ladies and gentlemen to do on the bridge. Like, "The ladies…blow their noses!" or "The gentlemen…throw up!" instead of the usual staid ladies curtsying and gentlemen bowing. Then Jean-Philippe laughed so hard that he gave himself the hiccups and they had to take a break.

When Alain checked his watch, he was truly shocked to see that over an hour had passed while they had been singing. Veronica really did play well, with light, graceful fingers that tripped over the keys. She seemed able to learn anything they threw at her. Even better than her playing was her voice. He would have guessed she might be a soprano, but instead, she had a rich alto tone like golden honey. The three of them seemed to blend beautifully together, but as soon as he had that thought, he felt the familiar bite of guilt.

Surprised at how much regret he felt, he cleared his throat.

"So sorry but I have to go now or I'll be late for my next meeting. I should have had my assistants cancel more, eh?"

He watched his little boy's face as he spoke, and Jean-Philippe first looked crestfallen, but then worse, he looked resigned. Alain tipped his son's chin up with a gentle finger, catching his gaze and holding it.

"We'll do this again soon, *mon chou*. I promise."

Looking more like a teenager than a preschooler, Jean-Philippe shrugged. "Whatever," was all he said, but Alain could hear the hurt under his words.

Alain looked at his watch again, and he was already going to be five minutes late, something he tried hard to avoid. Just because he was the boss didn't mean he was exempt from showing the respect he expected of all of his employees at every level. He sighed again.

"*Bon*, I'll see you soon. This was... I had a great time," he finished, turning on his heel before he said something even more insipid. Just before he left, he heard Jean-Philippe whisper to Veronica.

"This is the best, *best* day ever."

* * * *

That night, Jean-Philippe raced through his nightly routine, running straight into the bathroom after dinner and brushing his teeth and washing his face without Veronica even having to ask.

"Can't wait to get to bed?" she asked laughingly.

He shook his head. "Nu-uh, can't wait to hear more about Ludo and the beast. What's going to happen?"

Veronica beamed, thrilled at how much he was enjoying her story, and Jean-Philippe jumped under the covers so she could tuck the blanket tight all around him.

"The beast took Ludo back to his castle, where he fed the little boy a wonderful meal, the likes of which Ludo had never seen. In fact, Ludo thought he'd eaten better than anyone in his entire village, maybe even the whole kingdom. Then, the beast showed Ludo to a room of his very own, which was also something very unusual for the child. Ludo's whole family lived in one room and slept on a thin pallet on the floor, so lying on a feather mattress felt just like sleeping on a cloud.

The beast put something on Ludo's foot, too, that took the pain away. Ludo enjoyed every second, and the beast seemed surprisingly nice, but the whole time, a worry grew in the back of the little boy's mind. What favor would the beast ask in return? Ludo couldn't change his mind, though. He wouldn't. For all that he was poor, he knew the difference between right and wrong, and he always kept his promises. He'd learned that from his parents, and from his older brothers and sisters. Finally, when the morning came and he'd eaten himself full to the brim with delicious breakfast, the beast told Ludo what favor he would ask.

"'I am very lonely, Ludo. I wasn't always a beast, you see, but I was once a man until I was cursed to live as a beast. I would only ask that you tell the young maidens of your village that if there is one among them who will come and talk with me, only an hour every day, I will bestow great riches upon her family.'"

When Veronica looked over at Jean-Philippe, he was holding his eyes open by sheer force of will, but his eyelids were dropping lower and lower. She sat there for another ten minutes or so, watching him slip into a deep, peaceful sleep. She was about to get up and leave when she saw his pink bow lips twitch into a smile, then he chuckled in his sleep.

She thought maybe he was waking up, but no, his chest still rose and fell evenly. Then he said something, and she could just make out *blow their noses* before he went quiet again, still smiling. She had to smother her laughter with her hand.

In her own bed, she continued to have little-to-no spotty reception on her cell phone. Thinking of the tension and sorrow that seemed to hang around Alain like a fog, she found she was still reluctant to take another step to look up the circumstances of the accident. Now that she was coming to know Alain and Jean-Philippe better, as well as the rest of the household, it seemed increasingly wrong. She frowned at her reflection in the glass windowpane near her bed, which she'd gotten closer to as she waved her phone around the room, watching to see if she got more bars of reception. Upon further reflection, she thought she might be glad that she hadn't been able to look up the information earlier. Now, she thought she would leave it alone. If someone wanted to tell her the story of the accident, then they would tell her. She wasn't going to pry. Whatever had happened had clearly been very painful, and significant. If they…or, she mentally amended, *Alain*…felt she was close enough to them, then he would tell her. And if not, then she didn't need to know to do her job.

She flopped back onto the bed, more satisfied with her decision than she'd expected to be. When she fell asleep, this time there were no dreams or memories to interrupt her rest.

Chapter Eight

Over the next few days, they all settled into a sort of routine that everyone seemed to find mutually satisfactory. Veronica took Jean-Philippe on an outing every day, usually someplace they could walk to, although Monsieur Hormet drove them into town one morning as well. They had fun together. He was such an awesome kid that she thought it would have been difficult not to. Still, the highlight of Jean-Philippe's days, and Veronica suspected maybe it was the high point of her days too, was that in the afternoons, no matter where they were, Alain came and found them. When the three of them were together, the air seemed to crackle with excitement, and Jean-Philippe would practically bounce with enthusiasm and joy. Conversely, right after Alain left, heading back to a video or telephone conference, Jean-Philippe would grow temporarily quiet, withdrawing to somewhere within himself. At that time of the day, on several different days, he mentioned again that his mother and Sébastien were dead.

The household staff grew a bit friendlier, too, as they warmed up to her. She made it a point to seek each person out every day and to say good morning and ask in French how they were. It really was a small staff for such a large residence, so everyone was kept extremely busy, but she suspected they'd been chosen deliberately for their excellent attitudes and loyalty to Alain. They'd been friendlier, yes, but just like Monsieur Hormet on her first day, if there was even a hint of a personal question about Alain or Jean-Philippe, they became deliberately vague. The one odd moment came when she was seeking out Eveline in the kitchen because Jean-Philippe had changed his mind about what he wanted for his afternoon snack.

Just before she'd pushed the door open, she'd heard Eveline talking to Yvette. She hadn't been able to make out every word, and she'd felt like the worst sort of eavesdropper for hearing anything, so she'd made as much noise as possible. The words she had overheard, though, had sounded like *"No respect...relentless vultures...calling him the beast."* Both women had been flustered when she'd walked in, and it hadn't happened again.

Before she knew it, the day of her scheduled trip into Boston with Alain had arrived. Yvette was going to spend the day with Jean-Philippe, something she seemed much happier to do now that she'd had more of a break. Veronica could understand. She had quickly grown to adore the little boy, but she was looking forward to a little bit of quiet adult time herself. On the other hand, she wasn't quite sure if she was looking forward to or dreading having so much time alone with Alain in the car. Probably both, if she were honest.

In the gray light of the cloudy dawn, she looked at her reflection in the old-fashioned mirror on the dresser in her room. She tried to imagine what Alain saw when he looked at her, if he even *did* look at her. Her face was nice enough, with interesting gray eyes and cheeks that tended to turn pink easily, although she'd worn her hair the same way since middle school — long, dark and straight, cascading in a shiny mass to the middle of her back. She was just starting to get little smile lines next to her eyes and mouth, but she didn't really mind because she'd earned them — and was earning more by the day as she laughed and ran around outside with Jean-Philippe.

She made sure her clothes were always practical, neat and sturdy for playing with a preschooler, but even wearing the soft, purple sweater she'd pulled on that morning, likely the fanciest top in her current limited wardrobe. She wouldn't ever make the pages of a society magazine. She sighed, feeling hopelessly average for a moment, until she remembered the expression that would sometimes cross Alain's face when he didn't realize she'd caught him looking at her.

At first, she'd thought she was imagining things, being overly optimistic...projecting her own feelings onto him. But she'd looked objectively at him — or, as objectively as possible, anyway — and over the past couple of days, she'd definitely seen something soft and affectionate, something that made her breath and pulse speed up. It made her shiver in her most secret places. She knew it could still be nothing and it would likely come to nothing, but still...that softening and the excitement it made her feel was what made her hands shake that morning, made her half want to tell him she couldn't go after all.

Then her practicality kicked in. She was an adult, for goodness' sake, not some giddy teenager, and she was running out of clean clothes. She couldn't expect him to just keep buying her more. She had lunch plans with Katrin, too. She just needed to steel herself for whichever side of Alain she got today and to make the most of the time. With that resolve, she marched downstairs and promptly blushed when she saw how handsome he looked, even at this hour of the morning, waiting by the front door, immaculate in a gray suit more formal than anything she'd yet seen him wear.

Hormet had pulled up right out front in an enormous black sedan that she'd never seen before. Alain opened the door and helped her in, leaving heat wherever his hand brushed her, and she had to draw in a shaky breath as he walked around to get in the other side. Everything about him this morning was remote and elegant. Wealthy and powerful, he wore it as surely as he wore his custom-tailored suit. He even smelled a bit different, spicier. More expensive. But as the car pulled away, he flashed her a small smile, then he wasn't so strange. He was the same man who'd carried her on the beach and played the same song ten times in a row on his violin. But darn, did he clean up nicely. She had to surreptitiously wipe her palms on her pants.

"I apologize again for the early start. I didn't want to spend a night away if I didn't absolutely have to. This way, we should be downtown just in time to avoid the worst of the rush-hour traffic but still make my meeting," he explained, his rich voice filling the backseat of the car.

She nodded. "Of course. That makes sense," she agreed. She had expected him to lapse into silence, so she was surprised when he spoke again.

"Do you have any plans for the day? Maybe meeting a friend or boyfriend? We can come get you anywhere you'd like when it's time to leave."

She couldn't help but flash him a look of surprise at his question. "Just packing, mostly, although I am going to meet a friend for lunch." She took a deep breath. "No boyfriend at the moment," she added quickly.

Alain's face was impassive, as usual, but she thought she saw a gleam in his dark eyes, although she wasn't sure if he was pleased or just amused.

"Excellent," he said, and pulled several folders from his briefcase, but he didn't immediately open them. "I, er, thought that perhaps one of the men in the picture — the one on your phone — might be a boyfriend."

Of course he had remembered that. She shouldn't have been surprised that he'd asked, but somehow, she was. Part of her wanted to tell him about that day, about her brothers, but another part of her — the one constantly protecting her from the grief that always lurked close to the surface — won out. She just didn't know if she were ready to reveal that much of herself, especially since she wasn't even sure she could talk about it without her voice growing thick with tears, even if they didn't fall. She gave her head a brief shake in the negative and looked out of the window.

"Nope. Neither one," she said quietly, and she heard a rustling as he opened his folders.

They rode in silence for a while, and she took out one of the paperback books she'd put in her bag. She'd picked up a few when she and Jean-Philippe had gone into town. The bookstore on the small main street had an intriguing mix of local authors, serious literature and beach reads, combined with a bright and cheerful children's section that Jean-Philippe had loved. She was happy with her selection, quickly engrossed in the Gothic romantic mystery. She caught herself staring at Alain under her lashes more often than she'd like, and once or twice, she'd surprised him looking at her as well. She'd quickly looked down again, flustered, but her nipples had tightened and she'd had to shift uncomfortably at the heat she'd seen in his gaze.

After a little over an hour of quiet page-turning from her and page-ruffling and pen scratching on paper from him, she was almost surprised when Alain broke the silence.

"Hormet," he said in a quiet voice that carried through the car, "can we stop at the next exit. I was thinking we'd stop in for breakfast and coffee."

Food and coffee sounded good to her, but she hid a smile at his tone. He'd politely phrased it as a question, but with no real question mark. He was used to always getting what he asked for, and obviously, this was to be no exception.

Hormet inclined his head regally. "But of course. I took the liberty of calling Mrs. Hooper right before we left."

"Ah, very good," Alain answered, turning to Veronica politely to explain. "Mrs. Hooper is the owner and cook at a little gem of a café. She's not French, but" — he shrugged — "she could be," he finished with a small smile, which Veronica couldn't help but return. It was such a very French thing to say — a way to think.

When they pulled in to a quaint little downtown of a Maine seaside fishing village *cum* vacation haven and stopped before a small building designed to look like a Swiss chalet, someone had obviously been watching for them since a small, plump woman with rosy cheeks and gray, flyaway hair hurried out almost immediately with bags and a to-go tray of three beverages. Alain's face broke into a wide smile and so, Veronica was shocked to notice, did Hormet's. Alain rolled down the window.

"Mrs. Hooper, such a pleasure to see you, but you didn't have to come out. We would have come in." His voice was almost as warm as if he spoke to Jean-Philippe.

"Oh, I know, but Claude said that you were in a hurry on your way to an important meeting in Boston, so I didn't want to keep you one second longer than needed."

What the heck? This woman called Hormet by his first name? Veronica had nearly forgotten that he *had* a first name. Veronica had to stop her mouth from hanging open.

"Just so, although, Veronica, are you all right or do you, ah, need to stretch your legs?"

Again, Veronica had to hide a smile at Alain's uncomfortable tone. She assumed that he was really asking whether she had to use the bathroom.

"Thanks, but I'm fine," she answered, and he looked relieved.

Alain took the bags and drinks from Mrs. Hooper.

"I wasn't sure what the young lady would like, so I put in a little of everything, but don't worry, I put in four of the chocolate ones you like so much, just like your mother did." The older woman's eyes grew misty at that comment, then she gave a little wave.

Hormet jumped out of the car with a speed Veronica hadn't known he was capable of. "Let me get the door for you, Irene."

She blushed prettily and they went to the front of the small building.

Alone in the car with Alain, Veronica turned to him and raised an eyebrow. She did it without thinking, only then realizing that maybe it was a little too familiar a gesture for an employee to her employer, but he didn't seem to mind. In fact, his crooked smile made him look boyish.

"Mrs. Hooper was a friend of my mother's. They met when my parents would stay at the château. In fact, they would come over for dinner sometimes — Mr. and Mrs. Hooper — when I was a boy. Her husband passed away about five years ago, and Hormet was… Let's call it *delighted* to see her again when we came here."

Their combined laughter was loud in the confines of the car. The paper bags crinkled as Alain looked at their contents. "Ah, good. I see that she put in some of her cherry Danish, too. You should definitely try that, and maybe a custard tartlet, since I hear you like crème brûlée so much. She really is a genius with pastry. I'm guessing your coffee is probably black with just a splash of milk, the way you prefer."

Veronica stared at him wonderingly. When had Alain learned what she liked? She hadn't said anything, but he must have noticed.

"Just because my work keeps me from spending as much time as I'd like with my family doesn't mean I don't notice things," he said. His voice was mild, but she thought she detected a trace of defensiveness. "Anyway, I have spies everywhere," he added with flourish, and at that, she couldn't help but laugh. It was so unlike his usual austere manner.

Shaking her head, she took the pastries he held out to her. Mrs. Hooper had included china plates, too, apparently, and thick napkins.

"You know, I'm beginning to think that you are not at all what most people think," she said, then wished she could call the words back when all of the warmth left his face and it went back to its usual, careful mask.

"And what do you know about what people think?" he asked in a soft voice. That particular tone sounded dangerous.

Veronica raised her chin. She'd started this and she wouldn't be intimidated, not now that she'd seen behind the mask.

"I—" She broke off abruptly when Hormet hopped back into the car, a huge smile on his face, and his eyes soft with obvious affection.

"Irene—I mean, Mrs. Hooper—said to wish you both a safe trip and that she hopes you have a pleasant and successful day." He looked at them through the rear-view mirror, the corners of his mouth turning down into a small frown at their expressions.

"Thank you, Hormet. Here's your coffee and breakfast, and I'm afraid we'd better hurry so we don't lose any time."

There it was. Alain was back to his usual aloof, almost bored tone. Veronica wasn't fooled, though. Not anymore. There was so much more behind his façade. She knew he had to maintain a certain front publicly — if the press were watching him all the time, as well as business colleagues and society folks. It must be exhausting, but it made sense. What was odd, though, was that he felt the need to maintain it at home, too, with his most trusted staff and sometimes even with his own son.

If, as she was coming to suspect, Alain was the person people called 'the beast', what had earned him that name? What had started it? He could be gruff, certainly, and implacable, but what had made him that way?

Darting a glance at him from under her eyelashes, she saw that his expression was forbidding. Nope, she wasn't going to find out anything more now. Instead, she went back to her book and nearly moaned in pleasure at how delicious the flaky pastry was as it melted on her tongue. Mrs. Hooper was indeed a genius at pastry, and her coffee was delicious too. Black with just a splash of milk.

She was killing him. Slowly, and unintentionally, but he felt as if he might die of the slow melting heat she'd ignited inside of him. He had tried — with mixed success — not to stare at her reading earlier, but every time she'd bit her full lower lip or brushed a wisp of hair away from her forehead, he'd imagined himself kissing her, touching her. He'd had to shift and adjust himself in his seat so many times that he'd been certain she'd notice, but she had seemed mostly engrossed in her book. Not that she was immune to him — he'd seen the way she looked at him — but she was so goddamned innocent. Worse, she was an employee, and so should be under his protection. Not be a meal for 'the beast'.

Watching her eat her pastries, hearing her small moan of pleasure at the taste, every part of his body had come to attention. Feelings he'd thought were dead in him — or at least buried so deeply they could never rise again — came to surface. It was unnerving, being more alive than the half-life of sacrifice he realized he'd been living, yet he couldn't seem to regret it, either. Watching her throat work as she swallowed the coffee, he imagined her sucking his cock down the same way, and his blood heated in his veins.

As if she felt the predatory attention, she'd looked up at him then, and whatever she'd seen made her blush a deep crimson. Her mouth had parted and her soft chest had begun to move up and down rapidly. As their gazes had locked and held, he was no longer as certain as he'd been earlier that he could hold off on acting on the temptation of what they both clearly craved. If he couldn't, God help her. The beast would eat her right up.

After they parted ways in front of the tall high rise in Boston's Financial District where Alain had most of his meetings for the day, he paused before stepping into the golden revolving doors. He'd known he was being unfair to Veronica that morning, but he still hadn't been able to help his distrust. There was something about her that he found so charming that it was nearly disarming. When she'd smiled at him, inviting him to share her amusement at how Hormet had been acting toward Mrs. Hooper, as if it were the most natural thing in the world — as if he were the kind of man who were appealing instead of intimidating — he'd shut down. Out of defense. Because he didn't want her to see him that way. He was starting to like her too damn much. But he'd learned — oh how he had learned — that when he trusted anyone other than his family, it left him open to betrayal, and betrayal was inevitable.

He took a deep breath, feeling sorry for the people he was going to meet. It was a father and son who had spent their lives building their business, a small competitor to one of his company's divisions. He'd found out through someone in his network that the son, who had a young family, was going through treatments for a serious illness, and the father was having a hard time stepping back into the business after being semi-retired. They probably needed money desperately or they wouldn't have agreed to the meeting with him. He planned to capitalize on their weakness and to force them to sell, no matter what. This was what he did best, though. *This* was what had made him a feared and formidable force of business, someone to be reckoned with.

He would read the signals, the nuances of their expressions, until he had an idea of how much it would take — exactly how much — to get them to sell. It didn't matter that he liked the father or that he felt some sympathy for the son. This was business, and once his company had absorbed theirs, that division of his company would hold the dominant market share. He would make more money. They would all make more money, except for the several hundred people who would lose their jobs.

An image of Veronica and Jean-Philippe, laughing as they played and sang in the Music Room, popped into his mind, but he ruthlessly pushed it away. This was business and that was home, and he didn't need them to mix. He'd done that before and it had nearly gotten him and Jean-Philippe killed.

* * * *

"Sorry I'm late!" Katrin said next to Veronica's ear as she enveloped her in a cloud of her long red scarf and the perfume she favored. "There was a budgeting meeting that ran late, then I had to get a lunch for two of the principals—"

"Oh my gosh, don't worry about it!" Veronica cut her off. "You totally texted me. I got an extra half hour of sunshine on the Common, and you're here now. I ordered you a mocktail and I got us some fried pickles too."

"Oh my God, how do you read my mind? That sounds like the perfect thing!" Katrin settled onto her seat as Veronica sat back down, and her friend took a long sip of the frozen, fruity concoction Veronica had known she'd love.

"Mmm-m... So. Freaking. Good. I have now totally forgotten my rotten morning." Katrin smiled, and the expression made her pixie face look practically elfin. She was always complaining about being small and dainty-looking—everything her personality was not—but it was just her natural build. Combined with her short, flyaway blonde hair and deep blue eyes that were large and often sparkling, she was like a ball of contained energy, just waiting to bubble over. And she was adorable, but Veronica knew better than to tell her that.

"That sounds ominous. What happened?" Veronica asked.

Katrin took another long sip and waved her hand dismissively, even before she was done drinking. "Eh, just some work crap. Carla is avoiding assignments again then telling people that I'm the reason we're getting behind, but I think most people are wise to her game. Whatever. But I want to hear about *you* and what *you've* been up to! Who's your boss? What's he like?

Yummy? I feel like he's probably yummy or you would have told me more about him already."

Veronica let out a peal of laughter. "Don't you need to breathe? How were you able to say all of that in one breath?"

Her friend raised one light eyebrow. "Um, obviously I'm a superhero in disguise. Don't change the subject.

Veronica held up a staying hand. "Too bad you're not a mind reader, nosy-pants. Think of all the trouble it would save you."

"So true," Katrin agreed. "Alas, I have only been gifted with superhuman breath control and the ability to inhale fried food at an alarming rate, so..." she prompted, making a pushing motion with her fingers.

"The child I'm taking care of is just delightful — so, so much fun. I'm exhausted but happy at the end of every day."

Katrin inclined her head. "That's fantastic, but what about his father? He's a widower, right?"

Veronica sighed, surprised at how reluctant she felt to talk about Alain, even to her best friend. "He's totally gorgeous," she admitted. "Polite, polished, witty, obviously powerful with a healthy dose of arrogance thrown in, but...incredibly private. There are a lot of things he doesn't seem to want to talk about."

Katrin leaned forward eagerly. "*Oooh*, like what?"

"Um, yeah, I don't know, since he doesn't want to talk about them," Veronica returned.

Their appetizer arrived and they both took a moment to order, and when the waiter had left, Katrin whipped out her phone.

"Okay, we totally need to look him up. Give me his name." She looked at Veronica expectantly, her finger hovering over her phone screen.

Veronica shook her head emphatically. "No, I don't want to. I was going to…I would have on the first two nights if the reception were better up there…but now I want him to tell me. It would feel too intrusive to read about him, especially since I know how he and the other servants don't like the French press. He even thought I might be a sort of spy for a magazine when I took that picture on the first day… You know, the one I sent you, of the view?"

"What? Are you *serious*?" Katrin squealed. "He has, like, French paparazzi following him so much that they would pretend to be his son's nanny? He must be *really* famous."

Veronica shrugged. "I think he might be," she agreed. "It's weird, too, because everyone keeps talking about 'the beast' and I thought it might be an animal, but now I think it might be a man…probably my boss, like some really wide-spread nickname. But in spite of that fame — or maybe it's infamy? — somehow he's managed to keep his little boy really unspoiled. Jean-Philippe has a lot of stuff, but he's a good listener for his age and super curious. Like, he wants to go to the beach to look at snails and sea stars as much as he wants to go to the toy store. He mostly just wants to spend time with his father."

Katrin watched her closely, a considering look on her face. "You seem really happy — happier than I think I've seen you in a long time, especially with all that crap going on at your last job. They really used you like a slave. I think this new job is good for you."

Veronica thought about it. "Yeah, I've been feeling the same way. I didn't realize how much I'd missed spending time with kids. It was lucky Madame Montreaux thought of me."

"Yeah…it's awesome to see you so happy. And I guess I can live — under protest — without knowing any more about your mysterious Beast Boss, since you look so relaxed and satisfied. Now you can take some time to think about what you want to do next, too, without worrying about how you're going to pay the bills."

Veronica dipped a hot fried pickle into the zesty dipping sauce and crunched happily for a moment, savoring the salty, creamy combo, and Katrin did the same.

"Totally," she agreed when she'd finished chewing. "It's so much fun. Sometimes I feel like a bit of a fraud. The château is gorgeous, someone cleans my room for me, someone else cooks us delicious food and I get to do fun, educational things with Jean-Philippe all day. It's more like an extended vacation!"

Katrin raised her eyebrows. "Okay, yeah, that does sound kinda amazing. Maybe I should become an au pair. I speak German, you know. Well, I used to be a lot better, but I could brush up. Let me know if you meet anyone named Dieter or Hans or Fritz. Yup, a nice widower named Fritz sounds right up my alley," she joked, and Veronica shook her head at her antics.

"You think I'm joking. I'm not," Katrin deadpanned, before they both burst into laughter so that the people at the next table looked at them sideways. Veronica knew that Katrin loved her job, and was decidedly not very good with children, mostly due to a total lack of experience. Then their food came and they mostly talked about other, lighter topics.

Just as they were finishing, Katrin checked the time on her cell phone and made a face.

"Ugh…I wish I could stay, but it looks like I have to get back. Not all of us can be ladies of leisure, spending a weekday wandering around Boston, you know?" She pushed her chair back and stood as Veronica laughed.

"I do have to pack, but I'm not going to lie. It does feel kind of decadent to be free on a weekday in the city," she conceded.

Katrin pulled her large bag onto her shoulder. It almost dwarfed her small frame. She looked just as vibrant and pretty as usual, but something about her expression, maybe just around her eyes and mouth, made Veronica think something deeper was going on.

"Kat, is something wrong? You seem…sad," she spoke gently.

Initially, her friend looked like she was going to deny it, but then she inclined her head instead.

"Maybe…yeah, I might be a little sad, but I can handle it. I'll tell you more later. Promise me you'll go to a good reception spot at least every other day from now on. I have to make sure you haven't been gobbled up by the monster!"

Veronica made a childish X on her chest with her finger. "Cross my heart," she promised, smiling. "I'll talk to you soon!"

"Okay…travel safely with your hunky Beast Boss! Bye!" With that, Katrin spun and hurried out of the restaurant, leaving Veronica bemused and chuckling. Her best friend was a force of nature, but Veronica knew Katrin wouldn't pry, since she'd asked her not to.

Veronica paid the bill—she and Katrin had a standing practice of rotating who paid each time, and it was her turn—then headed to her apartment.

* * * *

She had finished packing a large suitcase and was just doing a little light cleaning when she heard a knock at the door. She'd expected Alain to call or send Hormet, but she should have known he would come himself. When she opened the door, Alain's large frame filled the entire doorway and her heart began to pound, as it always did. He smelled delicious, spicy and warm and masculine. It was a scent all his own, and one she thought she might be becoming addicted to. His face looked almost bored, but she knew him better now and saw through his mask. He was studying her apartment.

"Come in!" she invited, but she was surprised when he did.

"It's, ah, cozy," he commented, and she laughed, the sound filling the small rooms.

"Thanks for that, but there's no need to sugarcoat the truth now, Monsieur Reynard. It doesn't suit you. My place is kind of tiny, but actually, I was lucky to be able to afford a one-bedroom at all so close to downtown." She was proud of how homey she'd made it, but she was under no illusions.

Alain looked momentarily taken aback, then his face relaxed. "You're refreshing, Veronica. Dangerous to my peace of mind and maybe my business too, but...I don't know that I mind."

Veronica raised a questioning eyebrow at that cryptic comment—and how could she be dangerous to his business?—but Alain didn't explain, changing the subject instead.

"Do you have a fancy dress you'd like to show off?" he asked. Veronica's heart leapt into her throat, and she felt her breath quicken at what his question might mean. Or maybe because he looked so handsome, masculine and strong, filling every corner of her small living room until she wasn't sure she'd ever be able to look at it again without picturing him there.

"I...don't think anything I own is something you'd consider fancy, but I have a few nice dresses," she answered honestly, and a slow smile spread across Alain's face.

"There's that refreshing candor again. Would you be willing to put one on and come out to dinner with me? I'm having dinner with the governor of Maine in Augusta tonight, and I would truly enjoy your company. I was planning to drive straight there."

Veronica hesitated. He was in a strange mood, and she didn't know what to make of it, but she liked him like this — softer, somehow...younger, like the man she sometimes saw glimpses of on their outings with Jean-Philippe or in the Music Room. She didn't know if it was appropriate to go to a fancy dinner with him, though. After all, he was still her boss.

As if he could read her thoughts, Alain stepped closer, making her suck in a surprised breath. Every nerve in her body felt as though it came to attention in an instant.

"Don't worry, *chérie*. This will be an entirely staid and appropriate evening. Your only regret might be that you'll have to fight off falling asleep. Please, say you'll save me from the ignominy of nodding off into my own lobster bisque."

He looked charming, and somehow he managed to also look desperately in need of her help. That, combined with his nearness which made it hard to think straight, decided her.

"I'll go," she blurted out before she could talk herself out of it, and he looked satisfied, but unsurprised—as if he'd always expected her agreement, but he'd still enjoyed convincing her.

She went into her small bedroom after pouring him a glass of seltzer and went to the closet, already knowing exactly which dress she'd choose. She hadn't been lying when she'd told Alain she was sure her dresses weren't what he'd think of as worthy of showing off, but she did have one that she'd never worn and always wanted to. She and Katrin had been at one of the fanciest department stores downtown, looking through a sale rack just for fun, when she'd seen it—dark red, made from a soft fabric that draped beautifully and made the most of her curves without highlighting any of the parts she wasn't so crazy about, the color complementing her skin perfectly so she practically glowed. She'd splurged on the dress, even though it was totally impractical. Even with the discount from the sale, it had been expensive. But now, as she slid it on again, reveling in the way it caressed her skin before it settled onto her perfectly, she thought it had been worth every penny. She put her hair into a loose updo and, as she refreshed her makeup, brushing on some eyeshadow and pink lip gloss, she surveyed her reflection with satisfaction. She didn't know if she fit the part of the usual companion a mysterious French billionaire took with him to dinner with the governor of a state but still, she looked her best.

When she came out of the room, Alain's eyes flickered with surprise then…and she had to blink to be sure of what she was seeing…unmistakable interest— heat, even, that made her skin feel shivery and the core between her legs go liquid. She felt womanly and glamorous, and she did a little twirl to make the full skirt spin a bit.

When she looked up at Alain again, his expression had deepened, the lines around his mouth softening. His appreciation was still hot, but something more tender was in the back of his dark eyes, something that made a flush rise to her cheeks and onto her chest as well.

"*Lovely,*" he growled. "We'd better go before I make even more of a fool of myself today."

He grabbed her suitcase, only grimacing a little as he took the weight, even though it must be hurting his old injuries, and he opened the door, just brushing her back as she passed him. She felt his gaze on her as she locked the door, and again as he followed her down the stairs. She should have felt self-conscious, but instead she discovered that she liked it. She found herself putting an extra swing into her hips to make her skirt swish, loving that she could feel him watching her. Being the object of admiration and fascination of a man like Alain Reynard, however briefly, was heady stuff.

The spell continued as they got back into the spacious sedan, assisted by Hormet. The magic was only dimmed for an instant when Alain explained that he still had some urgent emailing to do before their dinner. She read a second novel—she'd finished the first on the way there—and looked out of the window, wondering what the evening would be like, but in the back of her mind, at every second, was intense awareness of his nearness. His warmth, his gentleness as he'd brushed her back... The little hint of gravel in his voice as he'd said, "*Lovely,*" with his slight accent.

They stopped briefly for coffee at a small place, different from the café of that morning. The view of the ocean was stunning, the sunset sky turning every brilliant color from light pink to dark purple. Alain made casual conversation about the weather, about Boston, how convenient the roads were, but there was a sense of anticipation. When his fingers brushed her, so briefly, she felt an almost electric current arc between them. Veronica thought perhaps it was mostly on her side, but then she caught Alain's speculative gaze on her more than once and she knew...she *knew*...he was feeling it too.

Almost before she knew it, they were pulling up in front of an enormous house. It was tall and stately, a classical grand home that looked like it had been built at the end of the eighteenth or the beginning of the nineteenth century. It was commanding enough just on its own, but it was set high up on a hill, overlooking the whole town, and every window blazed with light.

"Wow!" Veronica breathed, staring out of the window with wide eyes. "When you said dinner, I pictured a restaurant."

Alain chuckled and she loved the sound.

"It's quite something, isn't it? A jewel of your American Regency architecture. I'm sorry I didn't mention that it's somewhat of a banquet function for business leaders of New England or Maine or something like that. I don't often accept these sorts of invitations but this one seemed"—he paused and shrugged, pursing his lips—"*unavoidable*, I suppose."

"You don't like parties?" she asked, the words popping out before she considered that he might not want to answer.

His eyes grew distant, as if he were remembering something. "Oh, I like parties. I used to love them. It's the other guests I now find I can't stand." His laugh was humorless this time.

"It's lucky you invited me, then," she answered. He looked at her with surprise then his eyes softened.

"Indeed," he said dryly, but she knew he was amused.

Chapter Nine

Alain still wasn't sure what had possessed him today, first to act so uncharacteristically at his meeting earlier, then to invite Veronica to come with him tonight. He'd already spent hours with her in the car, after all. But the idea of going to the party alone had seemed pale and flat. When he'd had the idea to invite her, the evening had taken on a vibrant feeling of anticipation instead, and he'd wanted to get her to agree. Now, as he helped her out of the car in front of one of the most historical mansions in all of New England, inside of which waited some of the most influential local politicians and businessmen, all he could think about was getting a chance to see her spin around again. Even better, he'd like to get her alone.

That dress ought to be against the law, he thought, remembering how it had outlined her beautiful body and highlighted all her features. He couldn't believe that he'd ever thought her in the least bit plain. She had the curves of a goddess, and while her features might at first seem just pleasant, she had such joy and intelligence, such a sparkle in her eyes, that he couldn't look away. Now, that exquisite dress would distract everyone there, which normally would be fine with him, but he was included in the numbers of men who would be besotted, it seemed. Oddly, he felt an unfamiliar flare of possessiveness at all the male attention he felt certain she would receive. Perhaps inviting her tonight hadn't been a good idea, after all, but then he was taking her arm and it was too late to change anything.

When he darted a fleeting look at her face, excitement and wonder were plain. Her eyes flashed and her cheeks glowed. For a while, he'd worried that he'd never be able to feel happy again except with his son, but at that moment, watching Veronica's enthusiasm, the way she bit her lush bottom lip in the unconscious gesture he was coming to recognize, he felt genuinely happy.

When the enormous door opened, they were ushered inside by a young server to where a stately older couple waited, greeting guests. After they had both shaken the governor's hand and turned to his wife, Alain saw surprise then speculation flash onto the older woman's face before it disappeared underneath a polished hostess smile.

"Ah, Mr. Reynard, and you were able to bring a guest after all. How wonderful! You are very welcome, my dear!" She shook first his hands then Veronica's with both of hers. Alain had met the governor's wife a couple of times before and he secretly thought that her husband might owe at least fifty percent of his success to her incredible dynamism and tireless promotion of her husband.

"Thank you," he answered in his most charming tone. "My companion is Miss Veronica Carson. I hope we're not inconveniencing you—"

"Oh no!" she answered just as he'd expected, waving her hand dismissively, the large jewels on her rings catching the nearby lights. "Not at all! We're just delighted to have both of you here! In fact, let me take you around and make sure you know *everyone*!"

The translation of this was unmistakable, and Alain hid a smile. His hostess wanted to be sure *everyone* saw him. Alain knew he'd become somewhat reclusive over the past few years, since things had gotten strained with Joëlle, and he'd hardly gone out socially at all since the accident, so the governor's wife having him at tonight's party was quite a coup—one she was certain to make the most of.

He was initially a little worried about how Veronica would handle such an onslaught, and he regretted not considering that she might be miserable, but as they made a large tour of the room, making small talk with nearly every group, as though he were some sort of guest of honor, he watched her closely. To his surprise and deep pleasure, Veronica remained poised, friendly and utterly genuine, doing things like asking about what it was really like to be an artisanal cheesemaker, congratulating an older businessman on his son's recent admission to a small but well-respected private college and nodding with real interest as another businessman spoke at length about how he believed that lobsters might actually be immortal. She charmed everyone right before his eyes, drawing them in with her instant empathy and true caring for what they were saying—just as she'd drawn him in, he acknowledged to himself.

The casual touches between the two of them were driving him slowly insane. She brushed his arm, he touched her lower back, their fingers brushed as he handed her a glass of champagne from a passing server and he felt every contact all the way down to his damn toes. He had to adjust himself twice so that his growing hardness wouldn't be apparent to every guest there, and he couldn't remember the last time he'd been so aroused, especially by so little. Veronica was a little temptress, but she had no idea of her own potency.

At long last, their hostess was surreptitiously called away by one of her staff who had to practically drag her to whatever urgent issue was taking place. Before anyone else could join them, Alain put his hand on the small of Veronica's back and gently guided her to where he had seen a hall earlier that he thought led to the front balcony they'd seen as they pulled up.

He was right about the balcony, and the night air was cool as they stepped outside, but pleasantly so after the heat of the crowded room. This close to the ocean, the air was laden with moisture, too, and the fresh salty scent of the water. Veronica took a deep breath through her nose and turned a bright, grateful smile on him. If he had been another man, a better man, the kind with a heart, he thought maybe that smile would have captured it. Lucky for her, though, she was safe.

"Thank you!" she said. "I was beginning to think my cheeks were going to cramp up from the smiling."

Alain was taken by surprise at his own bark of laughter. "You didn't look like it," he observed. "Speaking as one seasoned networker to another."

She pulled a face that made him want to laugh again. "Ah, well, as the mayor's daughter in a small town, I spent a lot of years on my best behavior at parties. I learned that if you really listen, almost everyone has something interesting to say, something they want you to hear."

That explained it. "That's the first time you've mentioned your father. Either of your parents, actually. Why is that?" he asked. Something in her eyes made him add, "If they're gone, you have my sympathies."

Her small smile was sad, and he could practically see the inner debate on her face. Whatever the answer was, it had something to with whatever else she kept avoiding. The picture of her with the two young men on the beach... The sorrow that he'd recognized in her instantly, at first without even fully knowing what it was...

Finally, she gave a brisk little nod, almost to herself, and drew herself up to her full height, which was still much shorter than his own. He admired her. Well, he was growing to admire her for many reasons, but the way she tackled difficult or uncomfortable situations was on the top of the list.

"They're not gone...or, not in the way you mean. They got divorced five years ago and have both remarried. Now, they're both totally dedicated to their new spouses and stepchildren. My dad's involved in local politics in a different town now — or he was the last time I talked to him. We don't keep in touch much." The stiff set of her shoulders told him there was something more. Something important.

"What happened five years ago?" he asked, his deep voice quiet but still carrying in the stillness of the night air.

She drew in a shaky breath, and he put his hand over hers, which was icy. "You don't have to tell me, *petite*," he said. Even though he had been wanting to know the answer, had been subtly probing for it since he'd met her, he couldn't stand the sheen of tears in her eyes or the way her lips had a slight tremble. She shook her head jerkily.

"No, I think maybe I do. It's...important to understand...if you want to know me." It was a statement but also a question — and one he hastened to answer.

"I want to know you," he confirmed, surprised at the depth of how much he did want that. She was crawling under his skin in spite of him, maybe had already gotten there. He who was known for being cold and detached, emotionless and even brutal in the business realm, truly wanted to understand his son's young au pair. He was fascinated by her, drawn to her in a way that he hadn't felt in a long time — might never have felt, in fact. Joëlle had told him several times that he had no heart. No soul. No compassion. That not a single part of him was soft. But here was this earnest young woman proving that she'd been wrong. He wanted not only Veronica's body but all the rest of her, too. It was an unfamiliar sensation that he dared not examine too closely.

She looked out at the dark view, where the surrounding trees blended together in the pale moonlight since it wasn't a bright night. "I had a wonderful childhood," she began.

"I can tell," Alain answered. "You're quite spectacular with Jean-Philippe. You understand him. You know what's fun for him."

Her lips quirked up. "Yes, I think I do. I had two younger brothers, Gabe and Troy, and I spent tons of time with them growing up. We were like the three musketeers, three peas in a pod. Our parents called us 'the terrific trio' or 'the terrible trio', depending on the day." She smiled at the memory, her face soft and young in the silvery moonlight. Alain stepped closer to her, as if to give her his strength of his warmth, he wasn't sure which, and she swayed toward him. He thought her reaction was unconscious, and it made something hard inside of his chest melt just a little more.

"We stayed close, even when I went to college — not far away from them — and they came to visit me when I was studying in France. In fact, we'd planned a long visit. We'd travel all around France then go to several other countries, everywhere we'd wanted to see. They'd both worked extra at their afterschool jobs in town to make money for our trip, and we were having a wonderful time. We took that picture on the beach during that visit. It was just before — " Her voice quavered then cracked, but she pushed on determinedly. "Before Troy started not feeling well. *Really* unwell. He'd been unusually tired, but with all of the extra work and school and everything, we hadn't been that concerned. But when we were in Nice, he collapsed, and we knew something was terribly wrong. And it was." She had continued to speak, but two tears tracked silent streaks down her cheeks. "Cancer. Leukemia. We tried everything but...he died three months later."

Alain felt as if he'd been punched. How terribly sad, such a tragedy to lose one so young, a brother Veronica had obviously adored.

"I'm so sorry, *chérie*," he started, but she shook her head.

"You can't be nice, or I won't be able to finish," she answered. He understood. Sympathy, when genuine, could restart all the grief one had managed to set aside to get on with the daily tasks of living.

"Our parents were devastated — of course, we all were — so they grew distant from each other. And Gabe got this terrible guilt complex, so he joined the Marines, I think to take the most dangerous assignments they'd give him, but he says he likes it. And I—" Her voice roughened. "I miss them every day, every moment." There was silence between them for a long pause, an homage to her grief.

"Thank you for trusting me, Veronica," he said, and closed the last few inches between them to put his arm around her. She leaned her head onto his shoulder, where it felt like it fit perfectly, and they stood like that for a while. He wasn't sure how long.

The quiet was broken when they heard three distinct feminine voices drifting out of a nearby open window. Alain wasn't surprised that one was open. It had been growing stifling in the crowded ballroom.

"Can you believe she got 'the beast' to come to her party? That old biddy is going to be going on and on about this for months. Years, even. She'll be even more insufferable than usual."

Alain felt Veronica stiffen next to him. He felt hollow. Frozen.

"Well, he practically *had* to come or alienate all of New England, not that I think he cares. He has enough money that he doesn't need any of us," another, slightly lower woman's voice answered.

Then a third, this one higher, piped in. "That's for sure. You know, I heard he arranged for his wife's 'accident' and paid off the officials to get away with it. I don't even think those stories about him being hurt or burned are true. He looked just fine to me. Someone should warn that sweet young thing he was with that he's dangerous and that she should lay off the hors d'oeuvres, too." The three women laughed at that comment, the sound growing fainter as they must have moved away from the window.

Veronica turned a questioning look at Alain. It was obvious they'd been talking about him, and she would have had to be an idiot not to know.

"How can they ever think it's all right to talk that way about you and your wife? And call you 'the beast'? What really happened the night of the accident?" she asked.

Alain had never particularly minded his nickname. In fact, he remembered, as a young man, thinking that it was probably a good thing. Like a pirate, his name would inspire dread in people before they even met him. *'Ruthless,'* that long-ago reporter had called him. *'Like the fox that is his namesake, he's cunning, brilliant and vicious. A beast.'* The other papers had run with it, and soon there were articles on the fronts of French business and society pages about the beast's latest actions. Hearing it from Veronica's soft, pink lips, though, it sounded like blasphemy. He bristled, part of him deeply hurt at her questions, and the other part resigned.

"If you can't guess why, my dear, then I don't think you know me very well, do you?" he asked silkily. She flinched as if he'd struck her. Traces of her earlier tears were still on her cheeks.

"Why would you speak to me that way…in that voice?" she asked very quietly.

He didn't really know why, but he knew that he'd been expecting this from her all along—that she would be like all the others, like Joëlle—ready to believe the worst of him. He wanted to hurt her, too, so he lashed out.

"They were right, you know. Someone should have warned you about me. Now someone is. First, I negotiated much more generous terms than I ever should have for my opponents on the deal this afternoon—all because I was thinking of you, what you'd think and say. Then, I don't know what I was thinking, inviting you this evening. Let's call it an uncharacteristic lapse of judgment on both our parts and get out of here. You must have duties to attend to with Jean-Philippe."

The way her wide eyes flashed with hurt before she closed off her features should have been satisfying. He'd wanted to hurt her, and clearly, he had. But instead, he felt worse.

He ushered her back into the house, and after saying their brief goodbyes to their startled hostess, they were back in the car. They rode in silence the entire way, and she hurried to her room with barely a goodnight as soon as the car had stopped moving.

Veronica couldn't sleep. She lay in bed, tossing and turning until the covers and her nightgown were all twisted around her legs and she had to get up to fix them, heaving a sigh of frustration. The evening had started off so wonderfully, with her feeling glamorous and gorgeous, and Alain had really seemed like he'd been having fun too. Relaxing. When she'd decided to tell him about her family—about Troy—she'd truly felt she could trust him. Weirdly, she realized she still felt that way. But she didn't understand what she'd said or done to flip the switch from kind, funny, approachable Alain back to the beast he was known as. Of course, it was possible that being the beast was his true nature, with the relaxed, happy man as a mask, but somehow, every fiber of her being was telling her that the beast was the mask. The act.

Certainly, the gossipy and even catty comments that the women had made had obviously bothered him. But instead of getting mad at them, he'd turned his anger at her. For them to be repeating the rumors about his wife's death, though, even at a fancy party in Augusta, Maine, they had to be pretty widespread. It was difficult enough grieving privately. She couldn't fathom how hard it must be to have to do it publicly, with a young child, while defending himself against vicious rumors. And she was certain that was all they were…rumors.

Alain was a complex man, and he was not always nice, certainly capable of being tough. He wasn't violent, though. The father of one of her friends growing up had been a hard, cold man who enjoyed hurting his wife and children. She'd seen it in his eyes, and she hadn't wanted to play at their house until he'd finally gone too far and gone to jail. Alain wasn't like that. He might be scathing and cutting, but he wasn't cruel.

He'd been warming to her before. She knew it. The spark of awareness — the connection — she felt every time he was anywhere near to her went both ways. She was certain of that much. She decided that she would give it time. As though he were a bird with a broken wing, needing care but afraid to trust enough to get it, she would just continue to care for Jean-Philippe and she wouldn't push Alain. He'd either come around and trust her, since she'd done nothing to lose his trust, or he wouldn't. If he didn't, she suspected that some part deep inside of her, where no one had managed to touch her for a long time, might be deeply wounded, but it was too late to avoid that now anyway. And maybe she didn't want to. She'd spent so many years burdened by grief and sadness, afraid to let anyone new into her circle. That wasn't what Troy would have wanted, and it wasn't what she wanted, either. If anyone was worth the risk, she thought it was Alain. And Jean-Philippe? Well, he'd held a piece of her heart from the first moment she'd met him. She finally fell asleep with a smile on her face, deciding what adventure they should go on in the morning.

Chapter Ten

The next day, Jean-Philippe was overflowing with questions and excitement, as usual. She did her best to answer them as they went to breakfast, describing in detail her lunch with Katrin and the beautiful house where the party had been held. Yes, she'd had dessert. Twice. No, there hadn't been any horses...or camels. Well, not that she'd seen. No crocodiles either. Yes, it was possible they'd been keeping some in the basement, but it was highly improbable.

She was still smiling at the strange and wonderful ways Jean-Philippe's mind worked, even as she pushed on the door to the breakfast room with a gnawing dread and nervousness mingled with excitement. What would Alain be like? Would he still be coldly angry, or maybe, just maybe, would he apologize? But he wasn't anything. His chair was empty.

"So sorry, Monsieur Jean-Philippe and Mademoiselle Veronica. Monsieur Reynard had an earlier meeting he could not avoid. He sends his apologies." Hormet's tone was regretful, and his posture as he left the room with silent steps somehow conveyed an apology as well.

Veronica looked down at Jean-Philippe's disappointed little face and hated that she might have caused Alain to be absent that morning. Then she gave herself a mental shake. A man like Alain Reynard didn't avoid someone like his son's au pair. If he wanted to avoid her, he would have either ordered her to be someplace where he wasn't or he'd fire her. With all his wealth, power and influence, he didn't need to keep people in his household who he wasn't at least willing to tolerate. He must really have had something come up.

"I wanted to ask him about the crocodiles," Jean-Philippe said dejectedly, his shoulders slumping, and Veronica had to smother a laugh.

"Honey, I can assure you that your papa didn't see any crocodiles at the dinner party, either. I was with him the entire time, in the ballroom and out on the balcony, too, so we saw the same things," she assured the little boy.

His face lit up with interest again. "Ooh, did you see any ghosts in the dark?" Veronica opened her mouth to answer, but he continued speaking before she could get a word out. "I overheard my *Ton Ton* Marius tell Papa that he shouldn't carry the ghosts of my *maman* and Sébastien around with him. That he should forgive them. What does 'forgive' mean?" Again, with barely a pause, he lowered his voice and leaned closer. "I have tried to see them following Papa, but even when I squint like this" — he narrowed his eyes to blue-and-white slits — "I can't see them. I think maybe they're invisible or you can only see them in the dark. Did you see them last night? I miss them. My *maman* was very beautiful, did you know? And she always smelled nice, although I wasn't allowed to mess her up with my dirty hands, so I didn't get to touch her very often."

Veronica wasn't entirely sure where to begin with her answer. She wasn't sure why Alain should forgive his late wife and friend, but she could guess. Sadder than that, though, was the idea that Jean-Philippe had been trying to see their ghosts for Lord only knew how long. She knelt down onto the floor so she was at his eye level, and she put her hands on his shoulders.

"I'm sorry, but your uncle was using an expression. He didn't mean that your mom and Sébastien's ghosts were with your father. I'm guessing that they didn't know you were listening, huh?"

Jean-Philippe looked at her with wide eyes and shook his head. "No, they asked me to leave then closed the door, but it didn't latch all the way, so I could still hear."

"If they'd known, I'm sure they would have explained what they meant. There are no ghosts. I'm so sorry, honey," she said gently.

His little bottom lip trembled ominously, then his face crumpled into a mask of distress and sadness and his narrow shoulders shook with tears.

"Can I...hug you?" He gasped the question, and it made tears prickle in her own eyes. She couldn't believe he thought he even had to ask.

"Of course, honey," she answered, wrapping him in a tight hug until he calmed down, feeling her heart brimming with love and sympathy.

* * * *

Alain had wanted to set out that morning with Veronica as he meant to continue — cool and professional, totally detached, utterly unlike the unguarded sides of himself that he'd revealed too much of over the past week. Unfortunately, the press had seized upon some new angle of his wife's death in a front-page article that morning, and he'd had to get on an emergency call with Marius and Magali to discuss damage control instead. They'd spent an hour formulating a plan, only to have to revise it when yet another 'friend' of Joëlle's had surfaced, tearfully telling a story to the tabloids of how his late wife had been driven to an affair by his cold, emotionless demeanor.

According to her, and general opinion, he was never satisfied and had driven his wife to have an both an eating and a compulsive shopping disorder. In truth, he suspected she'd had both before he'd even met her, but he hadn't seen any of that. With the generous eyes of a totally devoted and besotted young man, he'd seen only what he'd wanted to see. It was after they'd married that she'd shown him her true self. The woman he'd loved and married had been nothing but a brilliant act, designed to catch him specifically. She'd acted like his dream woman because, as it turned out, it was his best friend, Sébastien, who had told her exactly what his dream woman would be.

He took several videoconferences in rapid succession while Hormet packed an overnight bag for him. He hated to leave any time since the fire, but he especially hated it now with things so unsettled with Veronica. However, no matter what, he trusted her to take excellent care of Jean-Philippe, just as he trusted all the other members of his smaller Maine household.

Her curiosity about his past didn't negate how deeply kind and understanding she was with his son. Hormet drove him to the nearby airport to where he kept a small jet for trips to New York or other destinations along the Eastern seaboard.

As angry as he had been the night before at the questions that Veronica had asked—and he still felt unreasonable fury well up inside of himself at the recollection—he realized that his last thought before take-off was of her, picturing her outside somewhere with Jean-Philippe, laughing in the sun. He wished he were going there, instead of to a gauntlet of interviews that promised to be uncomfortable at best and utterly miserable at worst. Why had she had to ask questions? Why couldn't she just have left things as they were? He could have continued to be Alain instead of the beast, and she could have been Veronica, not his son's au pair who could someday become a liability—a potential surprise new interviewee for next week's headlines.

He knew he was being cynical. She might well be just what she seemed—a bright, generous, funny, shy young woman who seemed unassuming at first but who grew more and more attractive the longer one knew her. The longer *he* knew her, in fact. And that was the kicker. If she wasn't drawn in by his wealth and power, wanting to know the lurid details of his past, then she was too good for him. He would just bring her down with all the baggage he carried. His anger. Mistrust. Unreasonably suspicious and cynical nature. Barely healed body. No, her questions had reminded him of the past that he couldn't escape. The gossipy women had been a stark manifestation of what he knew everyone was saying, what he would force anyone who got close to him to deal with.

On that unhappy thought, he leaned back into the deep leather seat and focused on how he would respond to all the interviewers in New York in person. He'd learned long ago that constant preparedness and practice made the rapid-fire interviews easier, more fluid.

He wasn't doing the interview for himself. If it were only his own reputation, or even just his family's, he would have flat-out refused. He wasn't there for the entertainment of the masses. His life wasn't a tabloid. No, he hated these damn things. But every time there was uncertainty about his leadership, their company's stock price took a dip. When opinions got really unfavorable, their stock plummeted. There were tens of thousands of company employees at hundreds of locations around the world whose salaries and livelihoods depended on him. His father had taught him that and, as ruthless as he was with the heads of companies, those who held the power, he'd never forgotten that he would have nothing at all if not for those hard-working souls, each one with their own families and concerns.

He started to rehearse possible answers out loud, pushing thoughts of Veronica and Jean-Philippe to the back of his mind, but they were always there with him.

* * * *

The next two days were very quiet with Alain gone to New York. Jean-Philippe had become his usual stoic self when Hormet had told them the news. They'd driven into town again, which had perked the little boy up, but even after he'd picked out a small plastic insect collection and two special saltwater taffy pieces, he'd still been a little subdued.

That night at bedtime, he'd begged for more of the story about the beast. He'd been sleepy a few nights and Veronica had been out, so the story hadn't advanced very quickly. But tonight he wanted '*lots and lots more about the beast.*'

Veronica had agreed, happy to do something to please him so much, and after he'd brushed his teeth and washed his face, tucked up with a shiny little face, snug in pajamas with flying pigs all over them, she settled into the chair next to him.

"Where were we, *mon petit*?" she asked. She knew right where they'd left off, but he seemed to love reminding her.

"Ludo had just told all the maidens what he'd promised the beast he would. He's a good boy who keeps his promises. I keep my promises, too. But everyone in the village was too afraid, except Ludo's own sister Anaïs."

"Ah, of course. You have a very good memory," Veronica answered, and Jean-Philippe glowed.

"Anaïs was Ludo's favorite sibling. She was the second-oldest and very brave. When the bull's pen had opened and the family's donkey had been right in its path, it was Anaïs who had run out into the field, making loud noises until she could close the pen before the bull could escape. She was pretty, too—at least, Ludo thought so. But none of the boys in town had wanted to marry Anaïs, tall and courageous as she was. Knowing what the future held for her if she didn't take a risk, Anaïs decided that if someone was going to go keep the beast company, it might as well be her.

So it was that she and Ludo set out two days later to return to the beast's castle. Their mother was crying, but Ludo had told such nice stories about the beast that Anaïs wasn't afraid. She imagined he probably did get lonely, alone in the castle. When they got near enough so she could see the castle gates, Anaïs sent her little brother home. Ludo didn't want to go, but he knew he had to do his chores, so he left Anaïs with a quick hug."

Veronica paused and, unlike other evenings, Jean-Philippe still seemed wide awake. She thought back on the evening.

"Did you take an extra chocolate cookie when I wasn't looking?" she asked, and Jean-Philippe nodded happily.

"It was just sitting there on the plate, and I knew it had to be for me," he confessed. Well, he didn't even confess. He was such an honest kid. He had probably known he should ask, but really, who could resist an unattended extra chocolate treat made by their fantastic cook? Veronica laughed and poked his nose with one finger.

"Well, Monsieur Reynard, you are supposed to ask before you eat any sweets. That cookie was *not* for you, and you had too much dessert today."

He looked like he might want to disagree, but he nodded his understanding. "Okay. I'm sorry. Now tell me more about Anaïs," he said eagerly.

"All right, just a bit more. Anaïs opened the huge wooden doors, which made a *creeeaaak* sound, like they hadn't been oiled in a very long time, and she thought the beast must not get many visitors."

"Like a haunted house?" Jean-Philippe interjected.

She inclined her chin. "Exactly like that. Loud and dark, but Anaïs was made of stern stuff. She'd grown up with little brothers and big brothers putting spiders and centipedes and worms in her corner of the pallet, so she was unfazed by a big, dark house. She heard a loud howl, which made goosebumps rise on her arms, and part of her almost turned back and left, no matter how lonely the beast was, but then she thought of how nice her little brother had said he was. She walked farther inside instead, forcing her legs and feet to move forward, toward the terrible sound. When she opened the door to the room the noises were coming from, her hands trembled, but when she saw what was inside, she ran in."

"What was it?" Jean-Philippe asked with wide eyes. Gauging that he still needed longer before she had a hope of him falling asleep, Veronica continued.

"It was the beast, and he had been hurt, with arrows sticking out of him. When she went to him and knelt next to him, he growled at her — a terrible, fierce growl, because he was in pain and he didn't trust her. He'd been hurt by people before, many times. Almost every time he'd dared to trust one, in fact, except young Ludo. But Anaïs was undaunted. She didn't shy away, but instead put a soothing hand on his uninjured shoulder and told him that she was going to find hot water and cloths and herbs, and she'd help him feel better. When she actually returned, he was quite astonished. He'd thought surely he'd scared her enough to flee so he could just be miserable in peace, but instead, she patiently tended to his wounds, never flinching at his snarls. Anaïs knew, you see, that sometimes what people or beasts do or say isn't how they really feel. It's because of how deeply they've been hurt before."

Jean-Philippe had finally grown drowsy during the last passage, and she waited quietly until she was certain he was asleep. He looked so sweet and young when he was sleeping. She kissed her fingertips and laid them softly on his cheek before she rose and left the room, only to jump almost a foot into the air when a deep voice spoke behind her.

"Were you reading that story?" Alain asked. She wondered when he'd gotten back. It couldn't have been more than an hour ago.

She stared at his face in the dim light of the hallway. He looked older and tired…almost haggard. She reached for his face without thinking, stopping herself before she touched him. He reached up one large hand and put it over hers, still outstretched, bringing it gently to the side of his face. She sucked in a sharp breath.

"I made it up. I've been making it up for him since the first night," she whispered. His cheek felt warm and scratchy from his five-o-clock shadow.

"You're a very kind person, Veronica. I'm not kind. Not at all." His voice was gruff.

"I think you are," she answered, and his expression softened. Grew tender.

"That's one of the things I like best about you," he said, and brought one of her fingertips to his lips, kissing it with incongruously soft lips. "I'm sorry but I do believe I may be overly sensitive on the topic of my late wife's death," he said. Veronica thought again that he wasn't someone who apologized easily or often, but this was the second time he'd apologized to her.

She had imagined him, many times over the past couple of days, realizing that she hadn't been accusing him of anything and apologizing. Although she hadn't imagined him kissing her hand — or maybe she'd wished he would, but she hadn't actually pictured it.

The reality was better than what she'd hoped, but she also wanted to be clear about what was happening.

"I can forgive you, Monsieur Reynard," she said, and his eyes gleamed.

"Call me Alain, *chérie*. I want to hear my first name in your voice. Hardly anyone calls me that, only those closest to me. I want you to be one of them."

Veronica felt a warm tingling start somewhere near her heart and spread throughout her body. He wasn't exactly saying that he cared for her and trusted her, but he was saying something very close to that. She thought that was enough of an answer.

"*Alain*," she said in a low voice. His eyes darkened and his mouth softened at the edges, making him look younger and gentler.

He leaned forward without warning, kissing her surprised mouth with a passion that made every fiber of her being thrill. He tasted like rich coffee and vanilla, and his spicy scent surrounded her, enveloping her, as his soft lips moved against hers. When he broke off the kiss, she swayed toward him, feeling lightheaded from the intensity and beauty of the unexpected gesture.

"I've been wanting to do that since the first second I saw you in that boxy suit, I think," he admitted. Then he heaved a deep sigh. "But now I think there are a few things I ought to tell you."

Chapter Eleven

When Alain had walked into the dark, still house, all he'd wanted to do was to see his little boy sleeping peacefully. After the hectic days, packed with stressful and antagonistic meetings with journalists who he generally considered to be among the lowest bottom-feeders, he'd needed peace. Uncharacteristic doubts that perhaps he'd overreacted to Veronica's questions had begun to creep in, which had made his mood even more foul. When he'd heard Veronica talking, he had gone closer to the door, not necessarily meaning to eavesdrop, but drawn inexorably to the sound. And curious, too, he could admit.

When he'd heard her story about the beast and the young woman who had healed him in spite of his trying to frighten her, his heart had felt as though it swelled in his chest. It was as though Veronica had been speaking to him, but there was no way she could know he was listening. She really did understand...maybe in a way that he hadn't.

He'd grown increasingly suspicious and cynical, but it had taken her gentleness and understanding to shine a light on why. Nearly everyone he'd known in his adult life had either betrayed him or tried to use him for their own gain, so he'd stopped even trying to trust. Instead, he pushed people away before they could disappoint him. He'd pushed Veronica away. But now he decided to pull her in. He would trust her more than he trusted anyone.

Half of him was horrified at what he was about to do, but the other half, the controlling half, knew that he wanted to try to trust someone again. He hadn't expected to feel this way — frankly, he hadn't wanted to feel this way — but now that he did, he wanted to go all in.

He led her down to his study, the room where he felt most comfortable. Surrounded by books and dark wood panels and rich brown leather, the room reminded him of his parents. His happy family life in his childhood. He motioned for her to sit down on one of the green velvet divans, and he sat next to her so his leg almost brushed hers — but not quite.

She looked up and held his gaze. "You don't have to tell me anything, Alain. You don't owe me your story."

He loved that she'd said that, and it made him feel even more confident that he was doing the right thing to tell her.

"Thank you, *chérie*, but I want to tell you. I might even need to. It's been…a difficult burden to bear. You, of all people, deserve an answer."

She touched his forearm briefly in understanding. "I understand," she said simply. "You can tell me whatever you'd like. I just didn't want you to feel obliged."

"I was honored by the way you trusted me, Veronica, with the story of your family and your brothers. My story, I'm afraid, doesn't make me look very good."

Veronica's face, when he stole a sideways glance, didn't look judgmental. Instead, she looked open and compassionate. He grimaced and began the story of the woman who'd brought him so much sadness.

"I loved my wife very much — or at least, I thought I did. She was exceptionally beautiful, like no one else I had ever seen, and she also seemed interested in the things that I found most important. When I was younger, I focused on power and expanding the business, making my own mark. I wanted desperately to distinguish myself from my father, and I wanted to make him proud. Joëlle seemed practically perfect, and we had a whirlwind romance. I gave her everything, anything she wanted — houses, cars, jewels, clothes... Everything. If I'd had any less of a fortune, she would have bankrupted me. But still, she didn't seem happy. In fact, after our wedding, she grew increasingly cold toward me. When she found out she was expecting Jean-Philippe, she seemed a little happier at first, but then she hated how he ruined her body — her words, not mine — and she never really grew to love him very deeply. She enjoyed playing with him, dressing him up and showing him off to her crowds of friends, but she essentially left him to me and his nanny."

He paused, remembering the small, outwardly delicate woman who had been his young wife. He'd learned that she had a stubborn center of pure steel, though. Her dainty femininity had hidden someone who was hard and selfish to her very core.

"To my shame, I didn't care by then. I had tried everything to improve our marriage, but she just didn't want to. She told me she refused, and that she knew I'd never divorce her, so we generally lived separately, only making occasional scheduled appearances in society. I didn't like how she was with Jean-Philippe. I have loved him since the first second I held him in my arms. He's been the center of my world. I thought that perhaps it was for the best that she stay away from him — and I loved him that much more."

"You were loving him for both of you," she said understandingly, and Alain drew her hand into his own, twining their fingers together. Her hand felt strong and warm, but the skin was incredibly soft.

"Exactly," he acknowledged. "The night of what we call 'the accident'... Well, most importantly, it wasn't an accident. There was a terrible fire at our home in Nice, set by Joëlle."

Veronica gasped, and Alain felt the familiar horror rise inside of him. When he'd realized what his wife had done and that Jean-Philippe was trapped... He had gone cold with horror, his stomach dropping out of his body before that same terror had spurred him to action.

"It was set in the family wing, where only Jean-Philippe and I slept. He was supposed to be spending the night with a friend, but he'd gotten scared and wanted to come home, so Hormet and I had picked him up. I will never know for sure, but I don't think Joëlle knew our son was home. If he hadn't been there and she'd succeeded, she would have killed only me. She wasn't a loving mother or mistress to the staff, but she wasn't overtly cruel, either. I think — and believe me, I've thought a lot about this — that she just wanted what she wanted. She perhaps wasn't even acting out of rage or hatred. I was the only obstacle standing between her and the fortune and power she always wanted more of. With me gone, she could be with her lover, Sébastien – my childhood friend and once my most trusted advisor."

Veronica's dark eyebrows drew together, and her eyes were filled with sympathy. "I don't even know how to express how awful that must have been."

Alain shook his head. It *had* been awful, but frankly, what had happened between them paled in comparison to the tragedy that could have occurred that night for Jean-Philippe.

"It was terrible, yes. Our little dog, Goliath, barely more than a puppy, was killed because he wouldn't leave Jean-Philippe's side. Jean-Philippe might have been injured or killed as well." His voice cracked and he felt a stinging in his throat at the recollection. He drew a shaky breath. "My sweet little boy might have died at the hands of his own mother. I don't know if Sébastien was aware of what Joëlle had done. Again, I suppose I'd prefer to think he didn't. He's gone now, so it doesn't really matter. That night, I was restless, *Dieu merci* – thank God. I smelled smoke, heard barking, which cut off abruptly, and tried to go to Jean-Philippe immediately, but the fire was set just between our rooms. I covered myself in a blanket that I wet down from the sink in my adjoining bathroom and ran across from my room to his. His injuries were minor, but at the time, we weren't certain since the smoke had affected him more quickly. I saw that the reason Goliath had stopped barking was because a large beam had fallen on him, crushing him." He paused, his voice cracking slightly. "I picked up Jean-Philippe's limp little form – not even certain he was still alive – and wrapped him in the blanket before charging out through the flames to get us both to safety. Unfortunately, some of the floor had burned nearly all the way through, so my leg went down into the broken, burning floorboards, and I had to crawl the last part, dragging Jean-Philippe. My leg had broken so badly that it was difficult to piece back together — that's why I limp — but I thank God every morning, with every twinge of pain or throbbing ache, that I somehow still managed to carry us to the clear night air."

Veronica held his hand in a tight grip — he thought she probably didn't even realize — and her eyes were wide. "I can't imagine how she could do that to you… How anyone could," she said in a horrified whisper. "Poor, brave Goliath."

"Thank you, *chérie*. He was a selfless hero, too good for this world. Don't forget that Joëlle paid a heavy price. She and Sébastien were in one of the cars I'd bought for her — her favorite, in fact. It was a clear night. Beautiful. I'll never forget how the stars looked above the burning roof of our home in Nice. The police reports confirmed that she was driving nearly two-hundred kilometers per hour. I think that's about a hundred twenty miles per hour. Was she afraid of being caught for what she'd done? Or just being reckless? I don't know what they were thinking, and I can't say that I deeply mourn the loss of my wife, but I certainly mourn the loss of Jean-Philippe's mother."

He sighed again, remembering how conflicted he'd felt when they'd told him the news in his hospital bed. He'd grown apart from her, certainly, but he'd never hated her. He still couldn't bring himself to hate the woman who'd given him such a wonderful gift in Jean-Philippe.

"Was Jean-Philippe all right then? Did he have any more lasting damage from the smoke?" Veronica asked, and Alain felt his heart squeeze.

His palms felt cold, and his whole body tensed. Could he do it? Could he really reveal the secret that only he and one private emergency room physician in Nice knew? He'd even watched the doctor remove it from Jean-Philippe's medical record before it was saved. It was something that had the power to make him feel a gnawing, persistent anxiety at nearly every moment, whenever it popped into his head.

"Are you all right? We can stop now. This must be incredibly difficult to talk about. To remember." Veronica's voice was soft and her expression was earnest. It was what decided him.

"Jean-Philippe is fine. *Now.* But at the time, it wasn't clear, and they were running a battery of tests to make sure. I insisted, in fact. I wanted to be certain he had the best possible care, that nothing was missed. Jean-Philippe's blood type…is AB positive. As his full-time caregiver, it's something you should be aware of."

Veronica watched him carefully. "Oh…kay," she answered, a little crinkle appearing between her eyebrows in the middle of her smooth forehead.

"Joëlle and I were both O-positive." He spat the words through gritted teeth, and he could tell she understood by the sequence of emotions that crossed her face in rapid succession. First was consideration, then her eyes widened in understanding, and finally, her hand tightened in his again in compassion, maybe even something more.

"Jean-Philippe isn't your biological son."

Biological son. He loved that she'd said that. No, Jean-Philippe couldn't possibly be his biological son, but he was Alain's son in every other way. For Alain, in every way that mattered.

"He isn't," he acknowledged. "I don't know if Joëlle was even aware. Jean-Philippe looks a lot like his mother, although now that I know that Sébastien is almost certainly his biological father, I'm surprised I didn't notice the resemblance before. He has his chin, you see. Now that he's a little older, he looks just like the boy I once called my best friend. It's the same chin Sébastien's mother and sister have."

Veronica turned toward him. "Oh my goodness, Alain. I can't even imagine how difficult that new revelation was for you, on top of being so badly hurt and losing your wife and friend in the same night. Did you lose your home there, too?"

He searched her face, his suspicious nature making him look for ulterior motives that just weren't there. Instead, he saw only concern, understanding and something softer. Something he wasn't sure he was ready to examine yet, but something that pleased him deeply.

"It can be rebuilt, but the family section was badly damaged. I haven't...cared to repair it. I suppose I should. My brother, Marius, might wish to live thereor my cousin, Magali. But it holds so many painful memories now, not just for me but the staff as well. I don't know that most of them would want to return, either. The ones who didn't come here have now all been sent to and settled at our other houses, depending upon their preference. Except Nanny Marie. She was our nanny, too—Marius' and mine—when we were children, and she loves Jean-Philippe very much. She had gone to her sister's to spend the night, since Jean-Philippe was supposed to be away. I don't think she's ever forgiven herself, and she was having a terrible time moving past what had happened. I finally convinced her to take an extended leave that has turned into a retirement — well-earned and deserved — and I think it has been the best thing for her."

Veronica nodded understandingly. "I can see that. That was kind of you," she said.

He shook his head forcefully. "I'm not kind, Veronica. I need you to understand that. Part of me is and will always be that ruthless beast that everyone calls me. They called me the beast long before everything happened with my wife, before I was married, even. It's in my nature, and it's what has made me so successful. In fact, thousands of people depend on me being that way in a business context to continue to be profitable."

She looked skeptical. "I've seen you, Alain. Truly seen *you*. Your face when you look at Jean-Philippe is soft and gentle — and most definitely kind."

Alain felt his lips quirk up in spite of himself.

"You've been studying me, huh? Does my face look the same when I look at you?" he asked, his voice going a little husky.

Her cheeks pinkened, though she didn't answer.

"That must be a yes," he teased, loving how her breath quickened and made her chest rise and fall more rapidly.

She didn't look at him as she answered. "I've noticed that your face does get softer, but there's something… I don't know, darker somehow when you look at me."

"Darker?" he asked, considering. Yes, he supposed it probably was. He was deeply attracted to her, not just her physical appearance but also her mind and spirit, her essence. But he'd been desperately fighting that attraction. "Yes," he acknowledged. "You bring out a bit of the beast, but in a good way."

Her already-pink cheeks went bright red at that comment, and it made her eyes sparkle in the dim light. Alain was enchanted.

"You seem to bring out a lot of uncharacteristic behavior in me," he continued, thinking back on his meetings in Boston. Instead of being his usual ruthless, emotionless self, intent on the best price, he'd actually backed off the father and son, striking a compromise deal. In the end, he'd still made an advantageous partnership for his company and a lifelong ally of one of his competitors where a hostile takeover might have decreased productivity all around due to the resentment everyone would have felt. "Although that may not be a bad thing. In fact, I like it very much."

She sat there, her hair burnished and shiny in the low lighting, her eyes sparkling and her cheeks rosy, quietly tearing down all the walls he'd built so carefully over the years. She took his breath away — this young woman who he'd initially barely seen — until she was what his mind turned to the most. He leaned forward and captured her lips with his again, taking her by surprise. As she parted her lips, he just brushed her tongue with his, and she went warm and liquid in his arms, leaning into his kiss until he never wanted to let her go.

He ran his hands up and down her back, reveling in the way his touch made her tremble in his arms. He brushed kisses down to her jaw, over to her ear and down her neck, feeling as well as hearing her gasp of surprise and arousal. She pushed her body closer to his until they were practically molded together, and still he wanted to get closer. His cock hardened almost painfully, and he groaned when he felt her softness against him as she strained toward him. It was the best kind of torture, but he practically shook with the need to tear her clothes off, right in his damned office.

Reluctantly, he broke off the kiss, but he couldn't resist reaching up one hand to tuck a gleaming strand of her hair behind her ear. He traced the top of her ear with his fingertip, and she shivered.

"I'm sorry, sweetheart, but it's getting late," he said, and her face fell. He sighed, adding the part he hadn't wanted to admit to. "And if we stay here like this, I'm not sure how much longer I'll be able to control myself. You look exquisite tonight, Veronica."

"I probably look frazzled from a long day with Jean-Philippe," she laughed, touching her hair, but he caught her hand and held it, along with her gaze.

"*Non.* You look stunning," he said, and he could tell she was pleased. "Plus, I think I like your hair wild like this," he added in a lighter tone.

Her lips curved up into a rueful smile. "Well, that's a good thing, because you can see it like this almost every day." She leaned forward, covering his hand with hers and making something warm and comforting rise from deep in his chest. "Thank you, Alain, for trusting me. It means the world to me." She stood and gave him a quick kiss on the cheek, enveloping him in her sweet, warm scent, vaguely reminiscent of peaches. It could barely be called a kiss, but he still felt it in every nerve of his body, and he fought the urge to pull her into his arms again and throw her down onto the couch.

"Good night, Alain. See you in the morning," she said.

"Good night," he echoed, sitting on his hands to prevent himself from going after her.

After she'd left, he took stock of himself, physically and emotionally. Physically, he was tired — exhausted from the grueling interviews and travel — and his leg was hot with pain and overuse. His cock was hard and aching, desperate to be inside Veronica. But he felt amazing, too, exhilarated in a way he hadn't felt in a long time...perhaps never. His lips still tingled from his brief kisses with Veronica, and he felt a boyish excitement and optimism that made his heart thump in his chest. Emotionally, he wasn't totally certain, but he absolutely felt lighter. Sharing the burden of the terrible truth — whole and unvarnished — with someone he trusted had made a difference.

On the flipside, even though he trusted her, he'd been hurt so deeply before that he couldn't help feeling nervous. What if he was wrong again and she betrayed him? He could destroy her, of course, but he'd given her the power to do a lot of damage to him...to his son. He truly didn't believe she had a malicious thought in her head, but he'd been disastrously wrong once before, with tragic consequences. Taking the leap and trusting her was exhilarating and terrifying, and he wasn't sure of the balance between those two emotions. One thing he was certain of, though. If she betrayed him, he thought it might cut deeper than anything Joëlle had ever done. He poured himself a brandy from the crystal decanter on the sideboard and sat up for a long time, trying to decide whether that was a good thing or a bad one.

* * * *

He'd kissed her, twice, and holy cow, it had been amazing. Mind-blowing. She wasn't even sure if the second kiss could be called that since it had been more of an R-rated full-on make-out session. Beyond that, he'd shared his deepest secrets with her. Veronica's heart felt full to brimming when she went to her room, and she was too excited to sleep. She lay wide awake with her whole body buzzing, in spite of the lateness of the hour. Instead, she held the memories of the end of the evening close to her, like the most beautiful gift, replaying every second from when he'd surprised her in the hallway to when she'd kissed his rough cheek and fled from the study. It was a cool night, but she cracked her window open so she could hear the sound of the waves crashing on the rocky cliffs. Standing right in the little pocket of breeze from the open window, she inhaled deeply, feeling invigorated by the scent of the cool, salty sea air.

Everything Alain had told her helped her understand how he'd acted—and even why he seemed to flip-flop from friendly to cold. He'd lost so much and been so deeply betrayed by those he should have been able to trust the most that it astonished her that he had even been able to attempt to trust her. She knew the pain of loss, the wishing that things were different, all mingled with the mix of guilt and gratitude at still being alive. She hadn't had to contend with anger, though, and no one in her family had ever tried to hurt her or her child. Still, no matter how it had happened, when you lost someone, it meant losing all the dreams you'd ever had involving them. Every loss had a ripple effect, like a pebble in a smooth pond. One stone caused waves all the way to the edge. Several stones and the whole pond sloshed around, at least for a while.

Now that she knew more about what Alain and Jean-Philippe had gone through, though, she hoped she could help him. She'd learned that having someone listen, like Katrin had listened to her, could be invaluable. Someone who was standing by, rooting for you and wanting you to feel better and succeed at anything was absolutely key to overcoming grief and loss and complicated betrayal. She could be that for him with no strings. In the back of her mind was the growing hope that this might be the beginning of something more, but she was realistic. She recognized that he was an incredibly wealthy, powerful man from one of the most prominent families in France, and she was a young American woman from the suburbs, temporarily working as his son's au pair. A couple of kisses probably didn't amount to very much in his world, whereas they loomed large and prominent in hers.

As she finally drifted off to sleep, she couldn't help the smile that tugged at her lips. Man, oh, man was he a wonderful kisser.

Chapter Twelve

That night, she dreamed of her brothers. It was a lovely dream, them running through a fair. A memory, in fact. Her parents had given her money for her and both boys and let them run loose on the Midway of their hometown carnival. She'd bought blue raspberry cotton candy and they'd all had blue lips and fingers from stuffing their mouths with the fluffy tufts of sugar that melted on their tongues. They'd ridden the spinning teacups and Ferris wheel, then the carousel, Troy's very favorite, at least three times. Every time they'd gotten on, he'd run straight for the tallest horse, and she and Gabe had taken horses next to him. As they'd spun, the lights and music had seemed to fill the night, until all she could see were her brothers' grinning faces, lit up with joy from within. It had felt like flying. When she woke up, for one brief instant, she was still there. Filled with the wonder and innocence she'd had in her teen years, secure in the knowledge of her family's love, surrounded by the brothers she cherished.

Then reality returned and a hard lump lodged in her throat. She pulled her knees up under her chin and cried silent tears that shook her frame and soaked a wet patch onto her nightgown. She'd generally gotten beyond grief this sharp, but sometimes a memory would still steal in, past her defenses, and take her by surprise. She cried for all that might have been — all the carnival and festival memories they'd never have, the man Troy would have become, the man Gabe might have become — probably softer and gentler, not cold and remote, running from his own grief.

Unbidden, some of the words Alain had spoken the previous night returned to her, about Jean-Philippe's chin. *'Like Sébastien's...just like his mother and sister's.'* Jean-Philippe had a grandmother and aunt who didn't know about him.

Of course, she understood why. To tell them would be to reveal that Jean-Philippe wasn't his biological son. She didn't know the legal implications, but even if it didn't call into question his guardianship, it would cause a monumental shift, most of all for the little boy himself. He'd had so much change in such a short time that it could prove to be too much, something that might scar him if not done exactly correctly. Beyond that, she could understand that Alain likely felt a great deal of resentment toward his former friend who'd betrayed him so badly, and by extension, probably his family as well.

But oh, another part of her wept for them. How much they were missing by not knowing the truth. If they hadn't been part of Sébastien's betrayal — and it certainly sounded like the other man had been quite a master of lies and deceit since he'd managed to convince Alain himself for so long — then they were just two innocents who had probably been devastated by Sébastien's death. She couldn't help but imagine if it were Troy who'd somehow had a child. No matter what, however he or she had come to be, she knew she would have loved the baby, wanted to be a part of his or her life as a doting auntie.

Her heart clenched, and she knew what she had to do. Even if it shook and maybe even severed the fragile bond she shared with Alain and tore at the strings of their connection and fledgling relationship, she wouldn't be being honest if she didn't mention it to him. Perhaps he hadn't fully considered the implications, which would be understandable. He was focused on himself and his son, along with their painful past with Joëlle and Sébastien. Sébastien might even have had knowledge of what Joëlle had intended. It was totally fair that consideration for those such a man had left behind wasn't at the top of Alain's mind. But she wouldn't feel right if she didn't say something.

If he was the man she thought he was — the man she admired and suspected she was coming to feel something deeper for — then he would hear her out. He might not agree with her, but he wouldn't let it come between them. If he wasn't that man, then she didn't think she wanted to pursue anything further with him. Unless she was way off target, he wouldn't send her away from Jean-Philippe for being honest and speaking her mind.

She didn't have a chance that morning during breakfast, which had been just her and Jean-Philippe, since Alain had had another early videoconference with some European reporters. After breakfast, she and the little boy headed down to beach again. It was a beautiful spring day, cool enough that she and Jean-Philippe needed heavy sweaters, but the sun warmed their faces, even as the sea wind whipped their hair. Jean-Philippe ran across the expanse of low-tide sand, hooting and chasing seagulls again. Every time he got too close, they flew to the other side of the beach, where he followed them, and the cycle repeated itself to his delight. The birds didn't seem to mind too much, either, since not a single one flew anywhere else. She sat on a blanket, watching the light play off the sparkling water, smiling at her young charge. He would probably have to take an afternoon rest. They didn't call them naps, since 'nap' was like a dirty word, but yeah, they were naps. She looked up to see a familiar, tall figure approaching her slowly. Raising one hand to shade her eyes, she felt a warm glow of happiness and excitement rise inside her. That handsome man had held her in his arms last night, had put his lips to hers, pressed against her. In the bright light of day, it was even more incredible.

An answering grin spread across Alain's face. He looked relaxed, the little lines around his eyes and mouth almost vanishing, and he was barefoot, wearing slacks he'd rolled up casually, and a thick sweater of his own. She noticed shiny scars on one of his legs, right down to his foot, and she realized he was trusting her yet again. He'd never shown her any physical evidence of his injuries before, except accidentally. Now he was quite literally putting everything out there. His dark hair was tousled, and his teeth practically gleamed white in his tanned face. She stood as he approached, and he put his large, warm hands on her shoulders, leaning in to kiss her softly on each cheek.

Before he pulled away, he whispered, "I'd like to kiss you more thoroughly, Miss Carson, since you look delicious, but I think we'd better not in front of Jean-Philippe." His eyes were warm, the brown flecked with gold, and his hand lingered on her hair for just a second longer before he pulled away.

She blushed at his compliment, and she agreed with his discretion. They shouldn't confuse Jean-Philippe, especially since she didn't know exactly what was going on between them.

"You look…" She paused, considering. "Happy," she decided on—and meant it.

"I feel happy. It wasn't, ah, easy to say the things I did last night, but I'm surprised to find I quite like sharing them with you, to be totally honest."

It was the kind of opening she'd been hoping for, since she really hadn't been sure how to broach the subject if it didn't come up naturally. She sucked in a breath and felt her stomach flutter with nerves.

He drew his dark brows together. "Uh-oh. That's a serious look. What is it, *chérie*? No regrets, I hope?"

Veronica bit her lip and shook her head. "Of course not, Alain. I'm honored that you trusted me, and I could never regret our…um, embraces," she stammered.

The brackets around his mouth deepened as his smile widened. "Our kisses. Yes, they were rather spectacular. I'm glad there might be more." His smile faded. "What is it, then? You should know by now that you can tell me anything."

She looked away, out at the water. "I had a dream last night…of my brothers."

He touched her shoulder gently. "I'm sorry, sweetheart. That must be difficult…bittersweet."

Raising her eyes to his, which were filled with warm sympathy, she continued. "It made me think of Sébastien's mother and sister. How much they must miss him."

He nodded slowly. "Yes. They always rather doted on him...maybe spoiled him too much. His father passed away when he and his sister were young, so it was only the three of them for a long time. His sister does a lot of charity work."

"Alain," she said, hesitating even though she was determined. He watched her face carefully. "I'm guessing that they would love to know about Jean-Philippe."

He stiffened and took an unconscious step back. For just an instant, she saw suspicion flash into his expression before it softened again.

"*Non, chérie*. I love how kind a heart you have and how you can feel so much empathy for those you've never met, but I can't. I *can't*. He's in every beat of my heart, the very breath in my lungs. If there is a chance this might harm him or jeopardize his life in which, now, he's totally surrounded by love, I can't take that risk."

The stark worry, mingled with a depth of love that was nearly painful to see, was written in every line of his face and body. She took a step closer into the warmth of his body and laid her head on his shoulder.

"Of course," she said, and she meant it. She understood where he was coming from. She might not totally agree, but she couldn't stand to see such a strong, powerful man—one so brave he'd risked his life, crawling through flames and dragging himself along a collapsing hallway to save his precious child— so unsettled. He'd given her the power to do this to him, to scare him and even to destroy him. She would never abuse it. "I was just thinking of them and how I would feel if I found out there was still some small continuation of a part of my brother out there somewhere, but of course you have to do what you feel is right for you and your son. I would never interfere."

He put his arm around her and squeezed, making her feel safe and breathless at the same time. "I know that, *chérie*. It's something I admire about you…your ability to see beyond the exterior straight to the heart of things…to the heart of a person. I appreciate your feelings, but this is something I'm utterly firm on."

His voice was still rich and beautiful, but his tone was like steel. She thought she might understand his nickname more. Woe to the man or woman who crossed the beast. She shivered in spite of the warmth of the sun on her face and his arm around her.

"Of course, Alain," she answered.

* * * *

The next couple of weeks were pure bliss, at least for Veronica, who spent nearly every day with Alain and Jean-Philippe. The weather was gorgeous as the early-spring melted into the late-spring, but even when it was pouring rain, they still had a wonderful time. The little boy soaked up knowledge from her like a dry sponge, and he could soon recite countless nursery rhymes and sing a bunch of traditional English folk songs, which the three of them had a blast practicing in the music room. Alain returned to his habit of joining them every afternoon, and he also joined them for dinner more frequently than not. She felt as if they lived in a beautiful bubble, separated from real life in a dream.

Every night after Veronica had put Jean-Philippe to bed, she and Alain sat up late talking in his study. He told her about his travels as a young man, what had made him want to take over the family business, funny stories about his brother and his cousin until she felt she knew them personally. She told him about studying history in college, how much she'd enjoyed studying in France and traveling around Europe and how Troy's death had put everything into perspective for her. Some things were important — health, family, friends, love — and some just weren't as important, as she'd always thought. She'd learned to never take a single happy moment or a lone breath, for granted.

Before she went up to her own bedroom, Alain would draw her into his arms and kiss her. He was always careful with her, but his kisses and caresses grew deeper and longer, and Veronica knew he was seducing her but taking his time. Veronica felt cherished and valued, and she admitted to herself that she might be falling in love with Alain, moody and brooding though he could be — and bossy as heck.

One evening, Jean-Philippe fell asleep earlier than usual. He'd been such a whirlwind that afternoon, running around in the sunshine nearly non-stop and taking only a short nap, that he'd nearly fallen asleep during dinner. When Alain had caught her eye across the dining room table, an electric sizzle of awareness had passed between them.

As she pushed the little boy's bedroom door closed behind her, holding her hand tight on the door itself as well as the knob to ensure that it closed nearly silently, she felt more than saw Alain come up behind her. He spun her around and slanted his mouth over hers in a passionate kiss, dark and commanding. Instead of his usual, coaxing kisses, this one demanded entrance, and his taste was spicy and hot. He pressed his body along hers, right there up against the wall next to Jean-Phillipe's door, and her nipples tightened where they met the hard wall of his chest.

"You're so beautiful, sweetheart. So sexy, soft, *mine*." He leaned his forehead onto hers, moving his hips almost unconsciously so she felt the hardness of his growing arousal pressing into her stomach. Her channel clenched in answering desire, and she felt goosebumps rise on her arms.

"Tell me you're ready to go farther, *chérie*. I need to touch you tonight, to taste you." His voice was husky and the hint of gravel in his tone stroked up her spine.

Veronica didn't need to think about it. She was ready, more than ready, to give Alain everything he asked for, maybe more.

"Yes." She breathed the word into his thick hair, as he trailed kisses with his hot mouth down the side of her neck, but she could tell he heard by the way he stilled for an instant, then went wild in her arms.

"I'll make this so good for you, sweetheart."

His growled words sounded like a vow, and she felt a delicious answering thrill in the depths of her womb. When he slanted his lips across hers again, it was a kiss of possession, so dark and rich that she could barely breathe, only conscious of the two of them. When he broke the kiss, their panting was loud in the quiet hallway. She felt almost dazed by passion, but Veronica was satisfied that he was at least as affected as she was.

He slid his hand down her arm to curl it around her fingers, and the quirk of his rueful smile was enough to make her heart do a little flip.

"Let's get out of the hallway, hmm-m? I'd love to take you right here, up against this wall, but I don't want our first time to be standing up where anyone could see." His eyes gleamed like liquid darkness, pieces of the night sky in the dim light.

She nodded, not trusting her voice, and he pulled her along with him to where she knew his bedroom was, at the end of the hallway.

She'd been near his room before but had never gotten so much as a glimpse of his private space, so when he opened the thick wooden door, it felt like something intimate. He had given her his secrets and now he was showing her, as well. It was his private, inner sanctum, and it suited him. The bed was an enormous structure of carved wood, and the bedspread was dark and masculine — plain, but with hints of silver and gold woven through that caught in the moonlight. The whole room was filled with his clean, spicy scent, and she instantly felt safe, surrounded by him.

When he reached to flip the switch to turn on the overhead chandelier, which also looked to be dark wood with candles and possibly some sort of antlers, she cleared her throat.

"Leave it off?" She winced at how shy she sounded. If she had been going for seductive, she was failing miserably.

He turned to look at her questioningly, and the movement made it so that they were practically touching chests. She could feel the heat blazing off him, and she longed to sway toward him, just another inch, to be back in his arms.

"It's not just our first time, but my first time, um, ever," she explained.

Somewhere, deep in the recesses of her subconscious, she'd worried that her revelation would make him hesitant, but it seemed to have had the opposite effect. His expression hardened into one of unmistakable possessiveness and deep desire.

"Such a beautiful gift you are giving me, *chérie*. One I will treasure, always."

He closed the gap between them, leaving the lights out so the room was only dimly lit by silvery moonlight, and he took her mouth again. She'd thought his kisses had been filled with passion before, but now he kissed her almost desperately, igniting an inferno inside of her that made her ravenous for more of his taste, more of his body. She molded herself to him, reveling in the contrast between his hardness against her softness. She wanted to be closer, touching him everywhere.

"I want your hands all over me, Alain." Her whisper was harsh, and he gave a strangled groan, walking her toward the bed and tugging at the hem of her shirt.

"Anything you want, sweetheart." He tore her top over her head, throwing it somewhere on the floor, and ran his hands up and down her back and sides, brushing his knuckles up along the softness of her stomach. "So soft, like satin. How do you stay so soft?"

The wondering tone of his voice boosted her confidence, and she thrust her chest closer to him in a wordless plea, which he was quick to answer. With a deftness that told her he had unhooked many in the past, he reached around to unhook her bra with one hand, and the lacy material went slack, sliding down her front until her full breasts bobbled free. Alain sucked in a strangled breath and stared at her for a long moment before covering both breasts with hands that were almost reverent.

"You're so beautiful, *chérie*," he breathed, and began to knead her soft mounds before tugging on her hardened nipples, making her gasp and squirm with rising desire. "*Mon Dieu*, you're sensitive, no? So responsive, sweetheart, that you're killing me."

She pushed deeper into his hands, wanting to feel more of his touch, and his chuckle was dark and rich in the quiet room.

"I love to touch you, Veronica." Then he bent his dark head and pulled one of her nipples into his mouth, and she nearly levitated right off the floor. The sensations as he sucked and tongued first one nipple, then the other, were like nothing she'd ever felt. She hadn't even realized that he was removing the rest of her clothes, then his as well, until she felt the cool night air from the open window on her overheated skin. She pulled back in surprise and her nipple dropped from Alain's greedy mouth with a soft popping sound that made her shiver.

Through passion-fogged eyes, she looked down at the man before her, all hard planes and harsh angles in the moonlight. He stood still for her study, tense. He looked like a medieval warrior, and she could easily picture him as a Norman conqueror, haughty and arrogant, with good reason. He had muscles everywhere, his chest, abdomen and roping along his arms and legs. And the proof of his desire for her rose, large and proud, pointing toward her.

"Alain, you're beautiful," she murmured, almost without thinking.

"Men aren't beautiful, *chérie*. And perhaps you can't see the scars in the light." His tone was harsh, but somehow, she knew he wasn't unaffected.

She shook her head. She'd never seen anything as gorgeous as his naked form. He was like a sculpture, but warm and loving instead of cold. "I know how you earned those scars. They only make you more beautiful."

He pulled her into a hug so tight that she thought he might crack a rib, and he rubbed his chin over and over the top of her head.

When he pulled away, she thought she might have seen the sheen of tears in his eyes, but she couldn't be sure because then he was kissing her again and laying her down onto the bed. They tangled there for a moment, his hands caressing and exploring every inch of her. She ran her hands over his body, as well, shy at first but then growing bolder. When she dared to reach down to stroke his thigh, his muscles hardened and he went still. He blew out a harsh breath and made a choked sound.

"I wanted to touch you everywhere, to let you touch me, but I don't think I can handle it, *chérie*. It's been too long, and I want you so damn badly. Say you'll open those sweet thighs and let me taste you?"

Veronica's face heated but she nodded. "Yes," she whispered. It was hard to overcome her modesty, but she let her legs fall open, and it was worth it to see the reverence and admiration stamped into every line of Alain's expression.

"*Mon Dieu*, *chérie*, you humble me," he said, and kissed his way down her body until she felt the warmth of his breath against her soft curls. He stroked a finger along her slit and she nearly bowed off the bed because it felt so good. She'd never had any hand besides her own there before, and it felt amazing. Alain was amazing.

"You're so wet for me, sweetheart, so ready for me to taste you."

"That's something you, um, *like*?" she asked tentatively, and he stilled, inches from her. "I mean, I've heard some guys don't, er, like a woman's taste…" Her face blazed with heat, but she couldn't take the question back.

He looked up at her and his eyes blazed, dark and hot. "Any man who feels that way is a fool who doesn't know what he's missing," he growled and bent his dark head. At the first touch of his tongue against her hot, liquid slit, she arched up and gave a little cry of surprise and wonder.

"Oh my God," she panted, and she felt as well as heard his chuckle against her pussy. He licked her over and over, stroking along her inner lips, tracing around her clit, and sucking and lapping at her juices until she thought she might be dying from pleasure. She thrashed her head back and forth along the bedspread, groaning and gasping, and without meaning to, she grabbed his head and was tugging at the silky strands of his hair, urging him or begging him, she wasn't sure. She only knew she needed more. She was so close to something, and when he rose onto his knees, she wanted to scream.

"Please, Alain, I need you. *Please*," she wailed, desperate for more.

"Yes, *chérie*, anything you want," he answered, his face still wet from her juices. He leaned over quickly to one of the side tables and she heard a crinkling as he pulled a condom on. When he rose again, kneeling between her legs, his expression was intense.

"Are you still sure you want this, *chérie*?"

Something inside her melted at the tenderness she could hear, underneath the harshness of his desire. "Yes, I want you. I want you to be my first, Alain," she answered, and she saw him shiver as though she'd stroked him with her words.

"If it hurts or you don't like anything, we can stop. It might kill me, but we can stop whenever you want, okay?" His voice was strangled but determined, and she lost even more of her heart at that second. She knew what the offer must have cost him.

"Okay," she breathed, and opened her legs again in invitation.

He covered her body with his, and she felt the crinkly, soft hair on his chest against her nipples as he positioned himself at her entrance. She rocked into him as she felt a delicious fullness as he began to enter her, a little bit at a time, stopping to look at her expression. The sensation of him starting to fill her felt good, so that she moaned, but the stretching became more painful. He pushed up against something inside her, and when he broke through, she gave a gasp of pain so that he held himself still.

"Do you want to stop, *chérie*? I think that's the worst of it, but we can stop." His tone was harsh and his breath sawed in and out of his lungs, and she thought that his arms might be shaking a little with the effort of holding himself still.

That offer made her warm inside, in spite of the stinging. She bit her lip as she took stock of how she felt. "I want everything with you, Alain. I think it's getting better already, if you could just keep going slowly?"

Despite the tension in the lines of his body, his expression was tender. "Of course, sweetheart. I'll go slowly until it starts to feel good, okay?"

He bent his head to suck one of her nipples back into his mouth and she felt her channel clench around him in arousal, so that when he began to move again, the sting slowly changed into pleasure. By the time he bottomed out inside of her, with all of himself inside, she was panting with desire again.

"You feel amazing, *chérie*. So tight and hot," he groaned, pressing his forehead to hers and breathing harshly.

"It fFeels so good, Alain," she whispered, then gasped when he flexed his hips slightly. "Yes, oh my gosh, I didn't know it would feel like this," she confessed.

Her words seemed to give him all he needed to start moving, still very slowly at first, watching her face intently. The desperate arousal that had faded away almost completely at the pain of his entry returned with his movements until she was nearly frantic again. She ran her nails up his back with each thrust, reveling in the incredible pleasure, loving the sound of him moving against her, within her. He shifted his hips to change the angle and his cock touched something inside of her that sent her right over the edge so that she tightened around him and arched up off of the bed, screaming with the incredible pleasure that washed over her like a tsunami. He pumped into her with hard strokes as her channel undulated all around his length, then she heard his triumphant shout as he began to come as well while her sheath milked him. She was still twitching with delicious aftershocks as he collapsed against her, his body sheened with sweat. Their breathing was loud in the quiet room, and she thought she'd never felt so relaxed or so close to another human being.

Her mind was totally blank for long moments — she couldn't have said how long — so that she said the first words that popped into her head. "Oh my gosh, Alain. Is it always like that?" She was instantly embarrassed, but his warm chuckle was tender.

"No, it is definitely *not* always like that. Any better, *chérie*, and I think I might not have survived. You're...incredible." He had gotten up briefly to take care of the condom but had returned almost instantly with a wet cloth for her, then snuggled up behind her, draped over her. She stroked her fingertips along his arm unconsciously.

"I had always heard that it was impossible for women to, um, you know, their first time." She felt his gentle laughter along her back as well as hearing it.

"Reach her peak? Find her pleasure?" he asked teasingly. "Or, in French, *jouir*? *La petite mort*?"

"We definitely didn't learn those words in French class," Veronica answered, smiling. She translated the second expression in her mind. "The little death? How funny...but accurate."

"Glad you think so, *chérie*. I don't know about any other virgins, but I wanted to make your first time so good that you would want there to be others." He chuckled, and she felt warmed from the inside out.

"Mission accomplished," she answered, teasing him in return, but then the rest of his comment sank in. "You've...never been with another virgin?" she asked.

"No," he answered, something in his tone warning her from asking anything else. Veronica realized, even as close as she felt to him, Alain had a past—a long history, in fact—with someone else. As much as they knew about each other, and as much as she was beginning to care for him and hoped he cared for her, there were areas that were still very mysterious.

She forgot all those melancholy thoughts, though, when he carried her to the bath before sweetly making love to her again before she went back to her room. This began the pattern for all their nights over the next week. Once Jean-Philippe was asleep, Alain would find her and they would make passionate love most of the night, tenderly, desperately, until Veronica had to return to her room for Jean-Philippe to find her there in the morning.

There were only two things that marred what would have been perfect happiness. After Veronica went back up to her own room, thoroughly sated by Alain's passionate lovemaking and feeling dreamy, doubts would begin to creep in. Jean-Philippe had innocently shown her a photo album, one that contained pictures—not many, but a couple—of his mother. Joëlle had been an incomparable beauty, someone who could have easily been a model or movie star based on her looks alone. Veronica wondered how she, cute but not lovely, usually dressed in pants and sweaters and boots for reasons of practicality with a four-year-old, could really compete with such a woman, even in death. Some part of her, the part that always thought she wasn't good enough in some way, the part that had been wounded and never truly healed when Troy had passed away and her family had all left her behind, that part just refused to believe that something bad wasn't coming.

When she managed to push those negative thoughts to the back of her mind, other dark thoughts would take their place, particularly ones of Jean-Philippe's aunt and grandmother. She didn't mention it to Alain again, and they both seemed to deliberately steer clear of the topic, but it was never far from her thoughts. She didn't know what they looked like, but she pictured the sister as someone who might look a bit like her, someone who grieved for her brother and had no idea that there was someone else out there. She fell asleep several nights with the tearful face of Jean-Philippe's unknown aunt in her mind's eye.

Chapter Thirteen

One weekday afternoon, when Alain had had to go into Boston, two visitors arrived. It was such an unusual occurrence — in fact, they hadn't had any social visitors since she'd been there — that Veronica was a bit thrown when Hormet came in to tell her. She jumped to her feet from where she'd been sitting on the floor with Jean-Philippe creating a complex jungle city out of blocks, and her heartbeat sped with nerves. Was it some brazen reporter, intent on a scoop? But why would Hormet have even let them past the front door?

Her relief made her a little dizzy when Hormet announced that one of the callers was Madame Montreaux and her companion was a Madame D'Abbey. Veronica had exchanged emails with Madame Montreaux when she'd first arrived, thanking her again for referring her for the position and telling her how much she was enjoying it, but it had been a few weeks. She asked Hormet to escort their guests to the informal parlor, where she and Jean-Philippe had set up for the day, since a steady downpour was falling outside. He gave her an inscrutable look, and Veronica had a flash of worry that perhaps she'd made a misstep somehow, but then she saw the familiar small form of the elegant Frenchwoman whose conversation circle she'd always enjoyed greatly, and she went to her with a smile to greet her with the two traditional kisses.

"*Tatie* Hélène!" Jean-Philippe cried excitedly, hopping up and running to the petite Madame Montreaux, nearly bowling her over. Well, Veronica thought, that explained it. He had called Madame Montreaux the affectionate term for aunt, like 'auntie'. Madame Montreaux hugged him, laughing, barely having to bend down since he was so tall for his age and she was so diminutive herself.

"Oh my goodness, look at how big you've gotten! You must have been eating your vegetables like we talked about — especially spinach and endives."

"Of course!" Jean-Philippe answered, flexing one skinny arm proudly. "Look at my muscles, *Tatie*!"

She examined his arm seriously. "Impressive." She looked up at Veronica, her faded blue eyes twinkling. It was funny, Veronica thought, to see her, impeccably turned out in a matching suit coat and skirt with a silk blouse underneath, not a hair out of place, being happily rumpled by the little boy. "I'm not really his auntie, but since I was his grandmother's best friend, I have an honorary title," she explained.

A movement behind her made them both turn and Madame Montreaux laughed again, raising her hand to her chest. "Oh my, and I am being unpardonably rude. Veronica Carson, may I present my dear friend, Josephine D'Abbey? Josette, this is the delightful young woman I told you about. She was a star in my conversation circle. Even Georges Mandier was impressed, and you know what a stickler he is. *Académie Française* this and *passé simple* that."

The other woman stepped forward, a striking older blonde with deep blue eyes that were both dignified and friendly. She and Madame Montreaux were clearly of the same generation, right down to their fabulous high heels and the diamonds that sparked on both women's hands and ears.

"Of course. It's a pleasure," she said in the throaty voice of an ex-smoker, which just made her seem even more French and glamorous. She embraced Veronica in the traditional French style. Oddly, something in her face looked vaguely familiar to Veronica, but she was certain she'd never seen the other woman before. She would have remembered.

"It's a pleasure to meet you, as well," Veronica answered, meaning it. She'd always liked Madame Montreaux, looking forward to their weekly coffee and conversation immensely in large part because of their leader, who always seemed to be able to spark good-natured debates. Any friend of hers would certainly be someone just as charming. And, after all, she'd trusted Madame Montreaux about the position with Alain, and she was loving every moment of it, brimming over with happiness.

"I'm sorry, though, that Monsieur Reynard had to go to Boston today. He's scheduled to be gone all day, I'm afraid," Veronica added apologetically.

"That is too bad," Madame Montreaux agreed, "but we planned to spend several days in the area — my late husband and I loved it up here so much that we bought a house, you see — so we can come back tomorrow."

"You're welcome to stay for coffee or tea. We'd love to have you, wouldn't we, Jean-Philippe?" Veronica prompted the little boy, who had wandered back to his blocks. He perked right up at the mention of his name, though, and came back over to them, holding out his latest creation.

"Yes, yes. Look at my boa constrictor! Isn't it huge? It doesn't have poisonous fangs but squeezes its prey to death. Prey is the word for animals it eats."

Veronica and Madame Montreaux exchanged an amused look, but when Veronica turned toward Madame D'Abbey, she'd gone pale, almost as if she'd seen a ghost.

"Madame? Are you all right?" Veronica asked, taking the older woman's thin arm and guiding her gently to a chair. Madame D'Abbey sat down heavily, as though she didn't know what she was doing. She kept darting glances at Jean-Philippe, who was oblivious, making animal sounds as his animal blocks battled each other. There was a lamp near him, and it lit his golden curls from behind, making them look almost gilded. Cherubic. Veronica didn't understand what had affected the older woman so much, though. When she turned back to Madame Montreaux, her friend and former teacher was staring intently at Jean-Philippe as well, her expression deeply thoughtful.

Just as Veronica was going to ask someone to explain, she heard the sound of doors, first the front door shutting then the distinctive squeak as the door to the sitting room, where they were, began to open.

"Veronica! Jean-Philippe! I finished early...actually, I told them I had to cut the meeting short. Really, I couldn't stand the idea of missing rainy-day songs with my two favorite people, so I decided to surprise you."

The door opened fully, and for one shining, beautiful moment, Alain looked only at her with such pleasure she thought she actually felt her heart squeeze. "What…?" he trailed off as he noticed the other people in the room, and his expression went from relaxed and happy to cold. Icy cold. It was as if his features froze, his eyes becoming hard stones, his lips tightening. In that second, a dark suspicion as to who Madame D'Abbey was formed in Veronica's mind with horrifying clarity, and dread was a yawning hole in the pit of her stomach.

"*Mon fils,* could you go see if you can find any of those little cinnamon cookies in the kitchen?" Alain asked in a carefully light voice, and Jean-Philippe jumped up immediately. He loved the cookies, and he often wasn't allowed to have too many, so he ran off happily to the kitchen, the door closing behind him with a resounding thud that made Veronica jump.

When they were alone, just the adults, Alain spoke again. "I see I've interrupted something," he said silkily. His voice was quiet and his tone was mild, but everything in Veronica shuddered. He sounded so remote, like he was talking to a stranger.

"Madame Montreaux and Madame D'Abbey arrived a short while ago. I told them they'd missed you, but invited them to stay for coffee or tea, of course," she answered, hating how breathless her voice sounded. She'd done nothing wrong — she *knew* that — but somehow she felt that it might not be enough.

For one millisecond, Veronica thought she saw something like hurt and betrayal in Alain's eyes, but then it was gone, and the only man in the room was the beast — utterly cold, heartless and devoid of feeling.

"I'm afraid I'm the only one who can invite anyone to stay, Mademoiselle Carson, and I think I'd like all of you to leave. Immediately." He executed a courtly little half-bow, oddly incongruous, given how hostile his words and posture felt. "Ladies" — he looked at the older women — "you must be tired after a long journey. Perhaps we can have this visit another day."

When he turned to Veronica, his dark eyes cold and dark, devoid of all the warmth and humor she'd come to expect and love — yes, *love*, she realized with a start. At the most awful, inappropriate time, she recognized that the joy and excitement, the total bliss she felt around Alain was definitely love. She was no longer falling in love. She'd fallen. Hard. But now that man, the one she'd come to care for so deeply was gone. A mocking, cruel stranger stood in his place.

"Mademoiselle Carson, I'm afraid to say that I don't think things are working out with you as a member of this household. Perhaps Hormet can drive you to the train station, and I'll ask Yvette to pack up your things and send them along as soon as possible. It's for the best that we all say goodbye now, don't you agree? I hope you have a safe trip, and I wish you good luck in your future endeavors."

"Alain, you're —"

He cut off Madame Montreaux's protest, whatever it was going to be, with a flick of his wrist. "*Non*, Hélène. This is not your affair." It was a testament to how often he had acted like the beast, perfecting the tone of absolute authority, that Madame Montreaux didn't contradict him. Instead, she shook her head and clucked.

"If this is what you want, we'll be happy to drive Veronica to the train station or anywhere she wants to go." She turned to Veronica. "Is that what you'd like, my dear?"

Veronica felt rooted to the floor, like her shoes had been nailed right into the historic hardwood. She couldn't believe that he was abruptly dismissing her this way, after all that they'd shared, all that she'd hoped for the future, without even asking for the truth. Sadness and disappointment were like living, breathing things inside of her, making her heavy. Then, underneath them, indignation swelled and finally, pride. She straightened her spine and raised her chin, looking him straight in the eye before turning to Madame Montreaux.

"Thank you, Madame. I would appreciate it. Yes, I'd certainly like to leave anywhere I'm no longer wanted." She drew a shaky breath. "Monsieur Reynard, would you please tell Jean-Philippe I'll send him a letter very soon?"

Out of the corner of her eye, she saw him acknowledge her words with a terse nod.

Then somehow, she wasn't even quite sure how because she couldn't remember forcing her legs to move, they were in the back of the roomy SUV that Madame Montreaux and Madame D'Abbey must have arrived in.

"Well, now, all that was quite a shock, wasn't it?" Madame Montreaux said, breaking the silence in the quiet interior. Veronica looked at Madame D'Abbey, who still looked utterly astonished. Her face was pale and her eyes shimmered with a sheen of tears, but somehow, Veronica could also sense a deep joy in the older woman.

"He looks so much like my son. It was like going back in time." Madame D'Abbey's tone was wondering, and she clasped her hands together.

Madame Montreaux put her hand over her friend's clasped hands. "He's grown into himself more since I last saw him. I can't believe... When he held out those blocks, it was as if Seb himself was showing us something he'd built." She turned toward Veronica, her eyes warm with sympathy. "I am sorry, though, my dear, that Alain assumed our visit had anything to do with you. Perhaps he'll give you the chance to explain once he calms down. He always had such a hot temper, well-hidden under that cold mask he likes to put up. He seemed so much lighter when he first arrived, happy."

Her words pierced Veronica's heart. She'd seen Alain's face when he'd spotted the two older women and the comprehension in their expressions. She knew how deeply Joëlle and Sébastien had hurt him, even though he wouldn't think of it that way. She thought it was unlikely that he would even want to step back enough to care about the truth, and maybe it didn't matter in the end. What would matter to him was that he'd told her his most closely-guarded secret, and she'd been a part of others finding out about it — others who might have a right to take his child.

She mustered a tremulous smile. "Maybe," she agreed. She was saved from telling any more lies when they pulled up to the train station, the same one where she'd gotten off the train on a few weeks earlier, excited and intrigued by what she might find, and who or what the beast could be. Now she'd seen him in all of his moods, from dark and angry to gentle and happy. He'd been *her* beast but for too brief a time. She felt a hot prickling in her eyes and the back of her throat.

"Thank you, Madame," she said to her friend, her voice thicker than she would have liked. She cleared her throat and turned to look at the smaller woman, the mother of the man who had been part of such hurt and betrayal for Alain. "Madame D'Abbey, you have my deepest sympathies on the loss of your son, and no matter how it came about, I'm glad you've realized Jean-Philippe's connection to you. Only please, I beg you, find it in your heart to consider how terrible it would be for both Alain and Jean-Philippe if you took him away."

Her words seemed to startle the other woman out of her shock and reminiscences back to the present, and her watery eyes shot up to meet Veronica's. "My dear, I wouldn't dream of doing such a thing! It's obvious Alain adores his son — always has, in fact. I remember that frightful Joëlle complaining about how devoted he was from the moment the boy was born. *Mon Dieu.*" Her voice cracked, and she took a deep breath to compose herself. "I know what it is to lose a child," she continued in a steadier voice. "I would never wish that on anyone else. No, I'd just like to be part of bringing even more love to a little boy who is obviously cherished."

The relief that Veronica felt wash through her was incredible, making her nearly lightheaded. She didn't know the woman, but the sincerity on Madame D'Abbey's face was unmistakable. Their moment of understanding was interrupted by the distant horn of an approaching train.

"I'd better go," Veronica said apologetically. "There aren't very many trains each day, and I...wouldn't want to be stuck waiting here." They all heard her unspoken implication, that she had nowhere else to go but back to Boston.

"Come stay with us, my dear. You're more than welcome, and we'd love to have you," Madame Montreaux urged, but Veronica shook her head.

"Oh, I couldn't impose on your vacation. No…I have to figure out my next move," she said. Mostly, she thought she needed to get away from everything to do with Alain, at least for a little while. She didn't want to be anywhere she might accidentally run into him.

"Thank you, and I wish you both all the very best," Veronica said, and hopped out of the car, hurrying to the train.

Alone on the train, once she'd hurriedly bought her ticket on the app on her smartphone, Veronica replayed the horrible scene in her mind, perhaps unconsciously searching for what she could have done differently. But she realized that for every choice she'd made, she would make the same choice again. She would have invited the two women into the house because there was no way she could have known one of them was Sébastien's mother. Even had she known her name, she wouldn't have known who Madame D'Abbey was to Jean-Philippe or to Alain. Madame Montreaux was obviously a beloved and close friend of the family, had seen Jean-Philippe at least several times and even she had never noticed the resemblance before. No, Veronica didn't feel badly about how she'd acted.

But she couldn't say the same about Alain. She understood why he was sensitive. Lord knew, he'd earned the right. He'd grown to look for betrayal and treachery around every corner, and so that was what he found. She knew that no matter what she'd said, he wouldn't have believed her because he didn't want to. And that was what made her eyes and throat sting again. She was just like everyone else for him — someone he didn't trust who would likely eventually hurt him. She'd thought she was growing to be so much more, or at least she'd hoped that. She'd let him into her body and into her heart.

Instead, he hadn't even listened. She could understand why he'd acted that way, but it *hurt*...so deeply. Her cheeks felt cold and she realized she'd been crying silent tears that traced down her cheeks and dribbled off her chin. She, who had thought she wouldn't have any tears left after losing her brother then essentially the rest of her family too in the aftermath. It seemed she could feel deeply again after all. Too bad she had to confirm it this way.

She picked up her phone to send a message to Katrin, but she was surprised to see an incoming message instead. Her brother had finally responded to her text from weeks earlier. Had it only been weeks? It felt like much longer to her.

Miss you too, big sis. Sorry...no phone before. Coming to Boston soon...love to see you.

She smiled in spite of her tears, realizing she probably looked slightly deranged if anyone was watching her, as she hugged the reply to herself. Gabe's words were just what she needed, and they were a reminder that, if she were patient and true to herself, loving and generous, she would always feel good about her actions. Someday, hopefully, that love that she sent out into the world would be returned.

She quickly texted back an enthusiastic agreement then, with a hand that was much steadier, she sent Katrin a quick message as well. Her heart might have been broken but her spirit wasn't, and she wasn't ashamed. She was sad, with an empty place where her heart used to be, but she would manage to keep going, somehow putting one foot in front of the other, and maybe, just maybe, things would turn out all right after all. Still, when she hopped into Katrin's car in front of North Station in Boston, her friend noticed she'd been crying.

Chapter Fourteen

Icy, righteous rage carried Alain through the rest of the afternoon and evening. How could she do such a thing to him? To his son? He'd trusted her — the first new person he'd dared to reach out to since Joëlle and Sébastien...since the fire. The first woman he'd kissed or made love to since the fire. No, he would call it sex. He'd never seen any sign of her plotting in her eyes, and he knew he'd been searching. Instead, all he'd ever seen were compassion, kindness, honesty. He really must have lost his knack entirely, because he'd read her all wrong. He felt like such a fool, canceling meetings and hurrying home just to spend more time with her and Jean-Philippe. He'd even been considering telling Jean-Philippe about his relationship with Veronica, of taking the next big step.

Ah, Jean-Philippe. Alain hadn't had the heart to tell his son that he'd sent away the young au pair. He'd simply said that she had had to go to Boston suddenly, which was, strictly speaking, the truth. But he'd left out that the sudden reason was that he'd sent her there. He'd felt a brief twinge, picturing her alone on the train without any luggage, getting back to an empty, cold apartment. But she deserved no better. He'd told her just how much it meant to him that Sébastien's family *not* know about Jean-Philippe's connection to them. He'd truly thought she'd understood, but her personal feelings must have overridden her promises to him. He could almost understand. After all, it was obvious she felt so strongly because she'd lost her own brother, and if it were anything but his own child at risk, he might have been able to forgive her. *But this…non. Non. Jamais. Never.*

He'd briefly considered that money could have motivated her, but even believing her to have betrayed him, he couldn't make himself believe she would have done it for monetary gain. She had tried to pay him back for the hideous hiking boots she'd purchased on that first day in town, even though their cost was utterly inconsequential to him. She'd never even asked him about her paycheck when he'd initially forgotten, for heaven's sake. Hormet had had to remind him. Hormet, who had been looking decidedly morose since Veronica had left. His servant's face, which was generally entirely impassive—sheer perfection for a butler—had actually been looking reproachful.

What puzzled Alain was how Veronica had gotten in touch with Madame D'Abbey within the past couple of days, since he'd announced his day trip to Boston. She'd been with him and Jean-Philippe nearly all the time, and there were very few locations where she could even get reliable cell service right at the château. Of course, she could have snuck into his office or sent messages to Madame Montreaux when she'd jokingly said she was sending more proof of life pictures to her friend, Katrin. She must have, he supposed, but it seemed...sneaky — sneakier than he'd really ever seen her being.

He steeled his heart to any doubts or regrets that might want to creep in and dashed off a quick message to his brother from his tablet. He was deliberately cryptic and urgent. They would need to talk about a legal strategy first thing in the morning. More, he'd have to tell Marius just how far Joëlle's betrayal with Sébastien had gone. Now that he thought about it, he realized he'd hoped that no one else would ever know that Jean-Philippe wasn't entirely his, wasn't biologically Marius' nephew, for that matter. He didn't think Marius would care — his brother loved the little boy and that wouldn't change — but Alain didn't want Jean-Philippe to ever question how deeply he was loved and wanted or whether he was a true Reynard.

As Alain passed Jean-Philippe's room on the way to his own bedroom, he could almost picture the usual bedtime scene — Jean-Philippe, his face shiny and rosy from washing, tucked in snugly, and Veronica, pulled right up next to him, her face alight with happiness as she spun a tale for the little boy. His heart ached. How could she have betrayed him, just like nearly everyone else had? What had she gotten out of it? He hoped it had been worth it for her because it had devastated him.

* * * *

"*Oh, la,* you look terrible," Marius said, squinting his eyes to look at Alain's projected image. Alain grunted in return. He'd seen his reflection in the mirror that morning. He looked awful because he felt awful.

"Okay, fine, don't answer. It must be really early there. You could have called me last night instead of sending a message, you know." Marius' voice, which had been teasing, grew serious. "I'm your brother. There isn't a time you could call that I wouldn't make work."

The uncharacteristically open words and the feeling behind them made Alain feel worse. He didn't know if he deserved them. He'd done a lot of thinking overnight, tossing and turning, and he was starting to have the uncomfortable suspicion he should have listened to what Veronica, or at least what Hélène Montreaux, had had to say.

Marius waved his hand in front of the screen. "Can you hear me? *Âllo?*"

The corners of Alain's lips twitched up in spite of his foul mood. Marius had always had a way of making him laugh, even when he didn't want to. Maybe especially then.

"I'm here, *crétin*. I just need more coffee…and maybe some advice."

His brother raised an eyebrow. "Advice? The beast asking his brother for advice? This I have to hear. What the hell happened?"

Alain took a deep breath. "Well, first, I have to tell you something that happened the night of the…fire." He deliberately said 'fire' instead of 'accident'. He needed to be honest, at least with his own family. Jean-Philippe would deserve to know the truth someday too, when he was older and could understand the complexity of the situation. "Then I'll tell you what happened yesterday afternoon, and I don't think I feel very good about it…about how I acted and how things turned out."

As he retold the story, leaving nothing out from Jean-Philippe's visit to the hospital all the way through kicking Veronica, Madame Montreaux and Madame D'Abbey out of his house, Alain heard confirmation in his own words that maybe he'd acted too quickly and harshly. Marius' reactions reaffirmed that suspicion.

"Oh, *mon frère*, what a mess. First, let's talk about my nephew, then we can figure out a plan for you to get Veronica back. You do want her back, *non*?"

Before Alain could answer, he heard a persistent knocking at his door. Deep annoyance flared—who would dare to come over so early in the morning, and why wasn't Hormet taking care of it?—then concern. When the two small women pushed their way in past Hormet—who frankly didn't look to be trying very hard to prevent them—he was curiously unsurprised. Madame Montreaux and Madame D'Abbey were both dressed to the nines, elegantly attired and perfectly coiffed and made-up. Their expressions both held looks of steely determination.

Alain narrowed his eyes and was about to order Hormet to get his top attorney on videoconference immediately when a bony finger, perfectly manicured, poked him in the chest. Madame Montreaux looked furious, but what really got his attention was the disappointment in her eyes, too. He shut his mouth and listened.

"Young man, you may be used to ordering everyone around, and I know you're very good at it, but I was there hours after you were born, when your mother was learning how to change your diapers. I held your hand at your first visit to the zoo, and I sat next to your parents, misty-eyed at your wedding to that viper of a wife. I gave you overnight to come to your senses, but now you can darn well listen to what I have to say." She darted a glance at her friend. "What *we* have to say," she corrected.

Alain couldn't argue with her logic. In fact, he'd already come to the conclusion on his own, so he shrugged. "Go ahead, then, *Tatie* Hélène. I was wrong not to let you and Madame D'Abbey explain yesterday."

Both older women looked stunned, then pleased. Madame D'Abbey stepped forward.

"You used to call me Josephine, when you and Sébastien practically lived at each other's houses." Her smile was a bit watery, but her spine was still steel-straight. "Thank you for coming to his funeral. It meant a lot to our family," she continued. He felt the familiar twist in his gut at the memory.

Alain gave a quick nod. "He was my friend. Before anything else, he was that, no matter what happened later."

Madame D'Abbey looked away, out at the gray morning through the window, seeming to compose herself before she turned back. "My son was many things. I know he wasn't perfect, and he made more mistakes than we realized, all surrounding your late wife, it seems...but we did love him. Jean-Philippe looks just like him. When I saw him yesterday, it was like going back in time and seeing my sweet, baby boy all over again, talking to me about sea creatures."

Alain felt sympathy for her. If, as he now suspected, Veronica hadn't called to tell her or Madame Montreaux about Jean-Philippe's parentage, it truly must have been quite a shock to see the little boy and how much he looked like her late son. However, he wouldn't allow his feelings to override his determination to keep Jean-Philippe, no matter what.

"I know you must have been thrilled, but I have to warn you—"

She cut him off by waving her hand. "Let me finish, Alain. Hélène and I spoke about this again last night after your Veronica asked me in the car, and it was one of the reasons we wanted to come over so early, to put your mind at ease. I don't want custody of your son."

The words hung there, and Alain feared his mouth might just be hanging open, too.

"You...don't?" he managed to ask.

Madame D'Abbey shook her head. "I spoke about it with Maude last night, and while she was delighted as well that she has a nephew and her little ones have a cousin..." She paused and held his gaze with her faded blue eyes, the ones he remembered so well from when she would play with him and Sébastien, running around their house and yard. "*Mon garçon*, as I told your Veronica, I've lost a son. I would never wish that kind of loss on anyone else. Jean-Philippe has been your son since he was born, and he always will be. We would like to see him sometime, to be a part of his life, but only to the extent that you're comfortable. When you've grown as old as I have and lost as many people, your perspective changes."

Alain's mind raced. Had he really been agonizing over nothing? Had the fact that two people very close to him had betrayed him made him so suspicious of others that he forgot that the true nature of most people was to be kind? He looked at Josephine D'Abbey—a woman who he'd once considered like a second mother, he'd seen her so often—and he realized that while she was still elegant and lovely, she looked older, and she carried the weight of sorrow like an evening wrap. She'd lost her beloved husband many years earlier, then she'd lost Sébastien as well. He wouldn't deny her the involvement she was asking for in Jean-Philippe's life. In fact, since his own parents had passed, and Joëlle's as well, Madame D'Abbey was Jean-Philippe's only living grandparent.

He took her hand into his own, her skin feeling thinner and more papery than he remembered. "Of course, Josephine. I don't want to tell him too much right away, since he's so young, but I do want him to know the truth at some point. I'd appreciate you and Maude visiting whenever you'd like. Maybe a trip to the zoo... He loves zoos and aquariums."

Both the older women smiled at him, and he saw the sparkle of tears in both of their eyes.

The sound of a throat being cleared made them all whip their heads around to look at Marius, who was still on videoconference on the large screen mounted on the wall.

"This is better than a soap opera," he drawled, and Alain couldn't contain his bark of laughter. Marius' smile was real, though. Alain knew his brother always had his back. On the heels of that relief, another thought popped back into his head.

"What did you mean, Veronica asked the same question? You weren't in touch with her about Jean-Philippe before you came here?" Alain felt balanced on a precipice, wanting to believe what his instincts were screaming, that Veronica truly cared, but not yet certain beyond a doubt.

This time, it was Madame Montreaux who answered. "*Non*, she didn't contact us, Alain. Oh, she emailed me to thank me for telling her about the position and to say how happy she was, but nothing about telling us to come visit or anything you'd apparently told her about Jean-Philippe."

The relief Alain felt at this final confirmation was only eclipsed by how foolish he felt. How regretful. He should have trusted her, listened to her. Instead, he'd sent her away in a hurry, back to Boston immediately and hadn't even let her pack her things or say goodbye to Jean-Philippe. He had done many things in the past to earn his nickname, but he'd never been more of a beast than he had been the day before.

He was so intent on his own thoughts that he almost didn't hear that Madame Montreaux had continued.

"…think she may forgive you. She's so in love with you. You're lucky, too, my boy."

He stared at Madame Montreaux, uncomprehending.

"What did you say?" he asked.

Marius chuckled on the TV screen, and both of the older women smiled as well.

"She told you, *crétin*, that your Veronica sounds like a saint. Even after you treated her badly — really quite shabbily — she was still concerned about you in the car yesterday. Sounds like she might be unfortunate enough to have fallen in love with you." Marius' voice was dark with wry amusement, but Alain thought he heard something else, too. Maybe…jealousy? More important, though, he heard what he hadn't dared hope for. Could Veronica really forgive him? Did she…*love* him?

With a jolt, he realized that he loved her, maybe had loved her from the moment he'd first seen her in that boxy, unflattering suit — maybe even before that, from the instant he'd heard her soft voice speaking so gently and kindly to his young son, friendly and sweet, just like the young woman herself. She was so wise beyond her years, understanding and patient with him, yet passionate and selfless as she gave herself to him as well. Lovely, inside and out. Her face rose in his mind, her cheeks rosy and her hair windblown, her eyes sparkling as they so often were, smiling. Veronica loved to smile. He felt an almost physical ache to see her again.

"*Mon Dieu*, I've been an idiot," he said, not realizing he'd spoken the words out loud until he heard laughter from everyone in the room, including his brother.

"Sure, but that's never stopped you before," Marius said.

Alain looked to the two older women. *Tatie* Hélène, someone who'd known him since the day he'd been born, was smiling indulgently. A small smile touched Josephine D'Abbey's face as well.

"Do you really think…? I mean—" Alain coughed, then cleared his throat. He was so confident in almost every area, but this area, love, was one in which he had failed spectacularly before, so spectacularly that he hadn't been able to trust, to even see, the wonderful person who had been right in front of him.

Madame Montreaux took pity on him. "Yes, I really do think she loves you, and she might forgive you. Now, what are you waiting for?"

A noise at the doorway made them all turn, and Jean-Philippe came in, wearing pajamas with jungle creatures all over them.

"Papa, I was looking for Veronica but I can't find her anywhere. Isn't she back from Boston yet? She's not in her bed, and it's all smooth, like she's made it already. Do you think she's taking a walk?"

Alain felt like the lowest of scoundrels at the hopeful note in his son's voice. He noticed Jean-Philippe was holding something behind his back.

"What do you have there, *mon fils*?" he asked, sidestepping Jean-Philippe's question for the moment.

Jean-Philippe's face lit up. "It's a surprise! We're working on it every morning and night. Well, except last night."

Alain crouched down. "Can I see it?"

Jean-Philippe shrugged. "I guess so. It's pretty cool. But it's a surprise, so we're saving it for when it's done."

Alain smiled at how artless his child was. It was probably a surprise for Alain, since it seemed unlikely to be for someone else. Jean-Philippe held out his hand, and Alain realized he held a book. It was bound with cardboard, and there was a lovely illustration in what appeared to be colored pencil on the cover. A fancy script, scrolling and graceful, printed "*The Beast in the Château*."

"It's beautiful," Alain commented.

Jean-Philippe grinned, moving closer. "Veronica did most of the cover, but I did some of the pages inside. Look, Papa. Well, except she did all the letters, but I did the pictures. Look… Look." He practically bounced on his toes, and Alain obliged by opening the book and flipping through the pages.

What he saw was an enchanting combination of his son's colorful illustrations with the occasional figure or object obviously drawn by Veronica, and the same beautiful script telling the story that Veronica had been telling Jean-Philippe every night.

The story had evidently continued, though, since Alain had last heard it.

"It's stunning, *mon fils*. This will be quite a wonderful surprise," he said gruffly, straightening again, a strange tightness in his throat as he read about how the brave and kind Anaïs had stayed with the beast, patient in the face of his rudeness, understanding when he was curt, sure within herself that he was acting so horribly because he'd been hurt in the past. When he flipped to the last page that had writing and a picture on it, it was a gorgeous illustration of what looked like a room in a medieval castle, complete with dark mahogany furniture, tapestries and a stained-glass window. It had obviously been drawn by a skilled and loving hand, and it looked familiar, although he couldn't quite place where he had seen it before.

"This is exquisite," he breathed. His eye was drawn all over the page, but particularly to the center, where two figures stood. The taller figure was dark and imposing but softened by the young woman with dark hair who stood right next to him with her head on his shoulder. The pose was touching. Sweet. Loving... The young woman loved the beast, and the beast loved her back.

Alain's heart thumped in his chest.

"We haven't gotten to the part where the beast transforms yet, but I think it's going to be the next page," Jean-Philippe explained.

"That *is* lovely. Your Veronica is a very multi-talented, it seems — although I suspected that already," Madame Montreaux commented, and Alain realized the two women had come to look over his shoulder. He was enveloped in a faint mist of expensive soap and perfume, and it made him think of his mother.

Madame D'Abbey nodded as well. "Very reminiscent of one of the galleries in the Bayker Museum. One of my favorites."

The spark of recognition that had been teasing Alain's brain flared to a full-blown flame. That was why it looked so familiar. He'd greatly enjoyed visiting the small Boston art museum in the past and had even donated a large sum of money to it at one point.

"Veronica loves art museums. She told me this gallery was one of her favorite places in the whole world. She's going to take me there someday," Jean-Philippe said proudly.

His words spurred Alain into action.

"How would you like to go there today? We can go find Veronica together."

Jean-Philippe nodded, the motion making his blond curls bob up and down. "Yes. Then we can finish the surprise!"

Alain chuckled. "Absolutely." He paused. "Or at least, I really hope so," he amended. He hoped so with every fiber of his being. "Let's go tell Hormet he can stop the quietly reproachful glances and drive us into Boston."

"Yay!" Jean-Philippe exclaimed, running in front of Alain to open the door.

Alain heard *Tatie* Hélène and Josephine D'Abbey wish him good luck, and he also heard Marius mutter, "Some beasts get all the maidens." He smiled, but he didn't stop. He didn't want to wait another minute to go after Veronica. He just prayed she'd forgive him. Again.

Chapter Fifteen

Veronica was proud of how she'd held herself together, but after a mostly sleepless night, she was feeling a little raw that morning. Katrin had stayed for a couple of hours the night before, gamely talking about everything under the sun except for Alain, making plans for Gabe's future visit. It had been fun, but as soon as her friend had left, Veronica's thoughts had turned right back to her very own beast. She'd tossed and turned for hours, reliving every moment of the horrible afternoon before, until she'd finally drifted off out of pure exhaustion, only to wake up a few hours later.

Even though she'd only had it for a few weeks — which shouldn't have been long enough to get so used to it — she missed Jean-Philippe's smile waking her up from a creepily short distance away from her face. She missed Hormet's stern exterior, which she was certain held a soft, gooey center. She missed Alain's morning greeting of kisses on her cheeks, and the passionate kisses he'd woken her with more recently. As that thought popped into her head, she sternly reminded herself that she wasn't thinking about Alain — not about his tall broad frame, distinguished face or how handsome he was when he smiled. She couldn't even handle the hint of the memory of how he'd made love to her, sometimes tenderly, sometimes fiercely. No…and yet, she couldn't forget how much it had hurt when he hadn't listened to her. She would never have betrayed his confidence about Jean-Philippe. *Never.* It made her feel sick — with an actual physical pain in her gut — that he thought she was capable of that.

She did what she always did when she needed solace. She sought refuge in beauty and peace, taking the subway over to the Bayker Museum so that she was the first person to go through the thick wooden doors when the security guard unlocked and opened them for the day. The familiar smell of stone and furniture polish mingled with the fresh smell of water and plants from the indoor fountain and courtyard made a wave of calm wash over her. No matter how dark things seemed or what she had lost, there was still beauty in the world. Beauty all around her. She just had to be sure to look. She'd been through agony before. Loss. Sorrow. She would make it. Only, did it have to hurt so much?

She went to her favorite gallery, the one that looked like a medieval castle, and she sat down on the bench there, slowly looking around at the treasures tucked into every nook and cranny of the room. She had always loved how the light coming through the stained-glass windows made a sparkling pattern on the stone floor, and the sunlight that morning was glorious. She was staring at the floor so intently that she didn't hear the other people enter the room until they were right next to her.

When she looked up into a pair of familiar chocolate-brown eyes, she thought she might be having a hallucination brought on by sleep deprivation. When a small figure pushed forward as well, laying a sticky hand on her bare forearm, though, she knew they were real and a stubborn hope rose and swelled deep within her.

"What—? What are you doing here?" she asked, looking from father to son.

"We came to find you," Jean-Philippe answered, and Veronica felt her lips twitch at his matter-of-fact answer.

Alain's mouth held the trace of smile as well as he looked fondly down at his son, but the apology and regret that she saw in his eyes when he turned his gaze back to her made her breath quicken and her heart speed up.

"*Mon fils*, could you please go with Hormet?" Alain asked, and Jean-Philippe scampered in the direction of the next gallery where Veronica could see the familiar figure of the older manservant. After his son was gone and they were alone, Alain sat down next to her on the cold stone bench. It wasn't a large bench, and she felt the warmth of his body all along her left side, but she didn't want to scoot over.

"We came to find you because *I* needed to find you," Alain continued where Jean-Philippe had left off.

Veronica turned to look at the painting in front of her instead of at Alain's face. He was so handsome, especially in the glittering light that filtered through the windows, that he almost didn't seem real.

"You didn't care to be near to me yesterday," she answered, unable to keep some of the hurt she'd felt from bleeding into her tone.

His large hand closed over her smaller one, engulfing it with warmth. "I was an utter ass yesterday."

Her gaze flew to his face, surprised at the bluntness of his words, at the honesty of his admission. He looked sheepish, and self-deprecating. She thought she might see the same hope that she felt reflected in his features, too.

"Go on," she said.

Alain chuckled. "I earned that. All right…you're still listening, so I'm feeling kind of okay. It was totally unfair of me not to listen to you and to assume that you betrayed my secret to anyone, especially without even asking you."

Veronica sat up straighter and held his regard "You hurt me," she admitted quietly. "It devastated me that you would think that, and even more that you wouldn't even ask me about the truth, especially after what we'd shared."

Alain sighed and lifted his free hand, scrubbing it down his face. "I'm so sorry, *chérie*. So very sorry. I realized my mistake. Honestly, I suspected I'd been wrong pretty quickly, but I was a little slow on the uptake. I realized that I've been holding back, just expecting some sort of betrayal. It hasn't been fair to you at all. I…know I have no right to ask, but…" He paused, and he looked pained.

Veronica held her breath, but she could still smell his unique, spicy scent.

"Can you forgive me? Again?"

She could feel his tension almost radiating down his arm and into his hand, the one that still held hers. Veronica thought of all the different scenarios she'd imagined and gone over in her mind during the sleepless night before, and she decided that this was better than all of them.

"The thing is," she started thoughtfully, and she felt Alain brace himself, "you were wrong, and I appreciate that you admit that. But life is too short, too precious, to hold grudges. I've truly never regretted anything I've done—only things I haven't done. You have to make me one promise, though."

Alain's face transformed from relieved to inscrutable, but he gave a brief nod. "Yes. Agreed. I will give you...*anything* you ask for." His voice was gravelly with the force of his emotions, and Veronica felt goosebumps rise on her arms.

"Just *listen* to us—listen to your family and friends—then decide. I think that the beast is amazing at business but not always so amazing at home."

Alain let out a slow breath and a rueful smile touched his lips. "Agreed wholeheartedly, sweetheart. I'm coming to grips with the fact that I'm not quite as perfect as I thought."

Veronica's answering laughter echoed off the stone walls and ceiling. "Did that hurt your mouth, for those words to come out of it?"

One side of his mouth rose in a lopsided grin, making him look much younger. Boyish. "Yeah, actually, it kind of did. Do you want to kiss it and make it better?" He waggled his eyebrows, and a burst of laughter escaped Veronica. She leaned forward and touched her lips to his. She meant it to be a short, light kiss, but the instant their lips met, she felt the same wild passion and tenderness as she'd always felt with Alain and she pressed closer. By the time she managed to draw herself away, she was flushed and rumpled.

He reached up one hand and touched his lips, his eyes darkening.

"May I ask you something in return?" he asked, his tone low and serious, all teasing suddenly gone.

Veronica didn't need to think about it. He wasn't perfect, but she trusted him. He was a good man, and he was the one she wanted. "Yes," she whispered.

"I don't know how things turn out between Anaïs and her beast, though I'll admit I hope they end well, especially since she has the patience of a saint, it seems—much like you do, sweetheart. No matter what happens between them, though, I know how I hope things turn out between us."

Veronica drew her brows together, not understanding where he was going until he slid down off the bench onto one knee. He didn't wince, although it must have hurt his injuries. Even though he knelt before her, she didn't quite believe it until he spoke again.

"Will you be my Anaïs, my queen, my love, my wife?" He held something out to her, but all she could see were his eyes, warm, dark and filled with something beautiful—filled with love.

Her eyes started to sting and his image wavered in front of her.

He looked concerned and raised one large hand to her cheek. "Too much, my love?" he asked, his voice tender.

She shook her head and smiled, the happiness rising inside of her until she felt like she must be glowing. "No, oh no. Not too much...never that, Alain. Surprise, yes, and pure joy, I think." She turned her face into his hand and kissed his palm.

When she looked at him again, his face had transformed. His eyes sparkled and his mouth was softer. He looked stunned.

"Was that a yes?" he asked. "I come with a battered body that limps, a drafty castle, a seriously bad reputation and a child who only stops talking to take occasional breaths, so you'll want to be very sure."

She chuckled at his description, then held his gaze with her own. "Yes. And I'm very sure. You're the beast I want."

She saw what he had been holding—a classically cut ring that looked to be an Edwardian setting of an enormous deep-blue sapphire surrounded by diamonds. It was stunning, but nothing was more beautiful to her than his happiness. He looked as though he'd just won the world, and she felt a warm glow at being the center of so much love. As he slipped it onto her finger, he whispered into her ear. "I will do my best to make you feel that way, *chérie*, every day for the rest of our lives."

Epilogue

"There's no room! Papa, you are taking up all the space next to Veronica!" Jean-Philippe complained loudly, and his father chuckled.

"She's my wife after all, so I think it's my right, don't you?"

Jean-Philippe stuck out a mutinous chin and shook his head adamantly.

"*Non*, she's my *maman*, too. It's official. I want to be right *there*." He pointed at the exact spot where Alain was currently lying next to Veronica on their enormous bed.

"Oh my goodness, guys! This bed is large enough to sail across the Atlantic Ocean on. I think we can all find a spot. Let me scooch over, and there will be plenty of room for you right here, sweet pea."

A bark of laughter escaped Alain as Jean-Philippe stuck his tongue out at him, curling up next to his stepmother in the spot she had freed up just for him. Veronica's heart soared to hear such happiness and levity from her beast and to see how much father and son were enjoying each other.

"Did you have fun with Granny Josette and Auntie Maude today?" she asked the little boy, ruffling his hair.

He nodded. "Oh yes, it was loads of fun. I got to meet my cousins, too, and we went to a zoo that has rides. It was super cool, although Granny Josette must have thought it was too expensive or something because she said it was definitely a once-every-two-years kind of outing."

Alain and Veronica exchanged an amused, secret smile above their son's head. Veronica could hardly imagine the stylish older woman at a combination amusement park-zoo. She would just bet that Granny Josette wasn't in a hurry to go back.

"Hmm-m, perhaps," Alain answered, his tone noncommittal.

"When are we going to start? This is taking *forever*!" Jean-Philippe continued, and Veronica couldn't help her laughter. She was trying not to encourage the little boy's flair for overdramatic pronouncements but…he was so darn funny. Alain hid a smile, too, and squeezed Veronica's hand. She felt a warm glow in the region of her heart.

"I'll open it now. We just got it back today, after all."

Looking down at the book, Veronica thought again how beautifully done it was. It turned out that the wife of the younger owner of the company that Alain had negotiated more generous terms with than he'd planned was an artisanal bookmaker. When Alain had called her to follow up and to see how her husband was doing now that he'd recovered from his treatments, somehow the subject of books had come up and Alain had worked out to send their fairy tale to be bound, officially. The kind woman, Hannah, had suggested that they would have a good shot of getting it published more widely, but Alain had told Veronica that he'd nicely refused, saying that the story was only for their family.

Jean-Philippe had been waiting impatiently for the 'Real Fairytale Book' to come back to them, and they were now reading its more polished form for the very first time, although she thought she could probably recite every single word in her sleep.

Veronica opened the book and rested it on her stomach, smoothing the first page with loving fingers.

"Once upon a time," she started, but was interrupted.

"Do you think the baby can hear, with the book sitting on top of your belly? I think you'd better speak up," Jean-Philippe suggested, real concern on his face.

"I think he or she can hear, *mon fils*," Alain reassured him, squeezing Veronica's hand again. "Listen up, little one," he continued, speaking in a low, loving voice, directly to Veronica's large stomach. She felt love and tenderness swell as they always did when he spoke to their baby that way.

"I'll speak up a little, too, though," Veronica added. "I mean, we want to be sure this baby hears the story of how kindness and love tamed the beast."

Alain's face spread into a wide grin. "Absolutely. The baby definitely needs to know that the beast and his family lived happily ever after."

Want to see more from this author? Here's a taster for you to enjoy!

Anywhere and Always: Falling for the Tycoon
Aurora Russell

Excerpt

The sky was a perfect unending blue, clear and brilliant, its beauty rivaled only by the magnificent expanse of bright aqua ocean and baby-powder-fine sand. It had always been Annelise's dream to see the Caribbean, and she knew she should have been happy. Ecstatic. Wasn't she still here, even if she was alone? But, instead, she just felt empty. Detached.

She'd cried her tears. So many tears. For weeks. Wondering what had gone wrong to make Kyle decide to walk out on their life together, ending their wedding and honeymoon plans abruptly. Wondering what would come next. Looking at the space where his toothbrush used to sit next to the bathroom sink, looking at the empty space in the fridge where the special espresso he loved had always been kept, she'd felt a gnawing, painful ache in her chest, raw like a sucking wound. She'd sobbed into her pillow, worried she'd alarm the neighbors in the condo above. Her hot tears signaled the end of not just a seven-year-long relationship, but also of her dreams for the future. She'd cried so much she'd gone numb.

She'd managed the chores of daily living—making food, getting dressed, going to work and to the store— but she'd felt like an imposter, like some zombie trapped inside the body of the vivacious, happy, hopeful woman she'd always been. She'd looked in the mirror and it had scared her. But still, nothing moved her anymore—not sadness, not anger, not understanding or judgment. Nothing. When the reminder from the travel agency had come through as an alert on her smartphone, the hot swell of anger had been as surprising as it had been fleeting. That spark was what had led her to do the crazy thing she'd done. Just to feel something, anything, she'd decided to take their honeymoon. Alone.

Logically, the decision had been clear. She should go—two weeks in a remote section of the Yucatan Peninsula, staying at an exclusive hotel right on the beach. It was a two-hour-long ride in a Jeep on bumpy roads through the jungle to get to the collection of luxury cabanas, perched right at the edge of a wild natural preserve. Quite a journey, but it was supposed to be worth it. This was her dream trip, and it was almost entirely paid for already…and non-refundable. When they'd booked it, she hadn't even had a nanosecond of concern about that portion of the terms and conditions. The idea that Kyle would have chosen not to go would have been laughable to her on that long-ago morning. After seven years of blissful love, she'd thought she'd known him inside and out. She had never been more wrong.

The decision to come had been more complex. Could she handle the possible emotional roller-coaster of going on what was supposed to be the romantic trip of a lifetime by herself? Was she crazy to risk putting herself through a possible ordeal of 'what-ifs' and 'might-have-beens'? But when she'd looked down at that small phone screen, slightly smudged from her fingers, and had again seen the hollow, eerie eyes in her dark reflection, she'd known. She was going to go. Her best friend, Marina, was the only one who seemed to understand and support her decision. Everyone else just looked at her like she'd lost her mind.

She hadn't been able to muster much enthusiasm for the packing, but still, even just knowing that she was packing to go had made her feel a little less frozen. Instead of staring at the same walls where she'd hung pictures with Kyle, or sitting on the same couch they'd spent several happy hours picking out at the furniture store, she would escape — or so she'd thought. But of course, she couldn't ever escape. Not really. She couldn't run away from herself.

So here she stood, looking at the prettiest view she'd ever seen, hands-down. The warm breeze ruffled her hair and the air held the delicate scent of tropical flowers mixed with the tangy salt of the ocean. Even the sound of the waves lapping onto the soft sand was exquisite. Soothing. And she could appreciate it all, but only in the abstract. Here in paradise, she was still frozen. Annelise sighed and turned, determined to keep walking until she began to thaw, even if it was just a little. Maybe seeing the jungle would help. She'd read there were even toucans. She sighed again, more heavily this time, trying to feel a glimmer of her usual optimism. Marina's voice replayed in her head, encouraging her. And with Marina's own past sadness, her advice meant even more.

'Go on, girl,' her friend had said. '*Don't let that man take one more day of your life. You have too much in you left to give. Go wild! Do anything and everything because you never know what's around the corner.*'

With those words in mind, Annelise doggedly continued, sinking her heels into the softer sand farther away from the waterline. It truly was incredible to be alone in such an unbelievably beautiful spot, and she hadn't seen another soul all day. She turned her face to the water again as she walked, watching as the sky lit up into a symphony of purples, pinks and oranges as the sun began to dip toward the horizon. Without warning, she fell over something large on the ground, landing squarely on a warm, hard object, which gave a startled grunt.

She scrambled up as quickly as possible, but not before she pressed up against the length of a tall, muscular man. He was warm and smelled of the ocean and the wind—and also a bit spicy, like some of the more exotic seasonings used in the local dishes. As she brushed herself off and stood as swiftly as she could, she just had time to realize that he smelled…incredibly good. *For someone I apparently fell on like a ton of bricks. Smooth. Real smooth, Annelise.*

"I'm so sorry!" she apologized, feeling a hot blush rise from her hairline to her ears and even onto her chest. She knew her cheeks must be flaming.

Home of Erotic Romance

Sign up for our newsletter and find out about all our romance book releases, eBook sales and promotions, sneak peeks and FREE romance books!

About the Author

Aurora is originally from the frozen tundra of the upper-Midwest (ok, not frozen all the time!) but now loves living in New England with her real-life hero/husband, two wonderfully silly sons, and one of the most extraordinary cats she has ever had the pleasure to meet. But she still goes back to the Midwest to visit, just never in January.

She doesn't remember a time that she didn't love to read, and has been writing stories since she learned how to hold a pencil. She has always liked the romantic scenes best in every book, story, and movie, so one day she decided to try her hand at writing her own romantic fiction, which changed her life in all the best ways.

Aurora loves to hear from readers. You can find her contact information, website details and author profile page at https://www.totallybound.com